Once Upon A Midnight Clear

An Enchanted Realms Novel

MICHELLE MILES

ISBN: 9798223670872 (ebook)
ISBN: 979-8-9898542-0-2 (paperback)

Rovenhe
Castle

Rovenheim
Village

R

Malvina's
Fortress

Grimbrande
Mountains

VENHEIM

For all those who believe in the magic of Christmas

Prologue

Christmas Eve, Present Day

Cold, hungry, and travel weary, Hilde stepped out of the taxi and into the gray slush by the side of the road. Without waiting for her to move, the driver took off, splashing her with damp snow as he sped away.

She sighed. Christmas spirit was not what it used to be.

Thankfully, she wore boots under her trousers to keep from getting wet, but her legs and feet were still cold. Stepping onto the freshly shoveled sidewalk, she made her way down the street through the old town in the fading light of day. As she walked down the sidewalk, she scanned the remaining open shops looking for that last perfect gift for her darling niece.

One of the shops, Elinor's Fine Linens and Things, caught her attention. Inside, beautiful scarves stacked along a table with a sign that read *Fifty Percent Off*. The bell above the door announced her entrance. The shop was small with one register toward the back. A wall of cubbies hosted folded sweaters. Pea coats hung in various colors on a rack near the sweaters. At the back wall was a variety of winter boots and shoes. Neatly folded scarves were stacked on the table in the center.

She paused at the scarf table. Some of them appeared to be handmade, knitted from the finest wool. She ran her hand over the top one in a beautiful shimmering pink. But pink was not her niece's favorite color. It was blue. A deep blue one with shiny thread intermingling with the chunky stitches caught her eye. As she held it in her hands, she closed her eyes and thought of the child.

Marigold was rosy-cheeked with bright blue eyes and ringlets of blonde hair framing her cherub face. She was bubbly and sweet and full of light. Since Hilde had no children of her own, she loved to dote on the girl, her sister's only child.

Hilde headed to the register with her treasure and placed it on the counter. The woman smiled as she began to ring it up.

"It's lovely, isn't it?" the woman said. "We sell a lot of these handmade scarves."

"It's beautiful," Hilde said with a nod.

"A woman in Scotland knits them from the wool of her own sheep," she continued. "I'm not sure why she started sending them to me to sell, but she wanted to make sure I always kept some in stock during the winter. Would you like it gift wrapped?"

As the woman held the scarf in her hands, Hilde swore she saw the wool shimmer in the low light of the shop. But, no, that was only an illusion. Even so, goosebumps broke out on her arms and skittered down her spine. Her gut tingled as she realized she was meant to buy that scarf from this shop on this day for a special girl.

"Ma'am?"

"Oh, yes, please. That would be lovely."

The woman beamed as she wrapped the scarf in Christmas tissue. She then tied it with an elaborate Christmas plaid bow and slipped a piece of holly in for decoration. She handed her the package and the receipt.

"Merry Christmas!"

"Merry Christmas to you, too," Hilde said, taking the small package.

She left the shop and started down the street. But something made her pause and glance back. The shop lights were off and the sign was turned to CLOSED. She must have been the last customer of the night. It was, after all, Christmas Eve.

There weren't many taxis at this time of night, especially on Christmas Eve after dark. She would have to walk the rest of the way to her sister's home. Lucky for her, Drumchapel Village, in which her sister's family lived, was quite close to the small shopping area.

By the time she arrived at the two-story house at 323 Crown Lane, her tired old bones were cold and weary. The white house was outlined in cheery holiday lights from roofline to ground. The bushes were covered in lights. Even the old live oak tree in the yard was wrapped. Everything about the house was magical.

Her sister really did love to decorate for the season.

She climbed the porch stairs, rang the bell and waited. Moments later, a shout from inside and then the door swung open. Her sister, rosy-cheeked and bright eyed, greeted her with a smile.

"Hilde, you made it." She waved her inside. "You look frozen."

"I walked from the shopping area."

"You *walked*? Are you mad? Give me your coat."

Before Hilde could put down the gift and slip out of the coat, Linnea was already pulling on the shoulders. She slid one arm out and then the other.

"Jack, Hilde is here!" Linnea called.

Jack, her brother-in-law, was busy snoozing in his recliner in front of a showing of *It's a Wonderful Life*. His response was a soft snore.

"He doesn't want to see me anyway. Where's my niece?"

"She's upstairs in her room. She's not feeling well." Linnea tried to hide the concern in her voice but failed.

"What's wrong with her?"

"I'm not sure. I thought I'd take her to the doctor after the holidays if she doesn't get better."

Linnea started up the stairs, motioning for Hilde to follow her.

Marigold's bedroom was the first one at the top of the stairs. Linnea opened the door with a flourish.

"Look who's here, Marigold." She waved to Hilde.

Sleepy-eyed Marigold blinked owlish eyes as she sat up in her bed. Her room was decorated for a small princess with pink walls and princess furniture. She had a canopy bed with twinkle lights strung up to give the room a warm, inviting glow. *Rudolph the Red-Nosed Reindeer* played on the television across from the girl's bed.

"Hi, auntie," she said around a giant yawn.

"Hello, princess. I brought you a gift." She handed her the small package as her sister exited the room.

"Can I open it now?" the girl asked. A bright smile was on her face.

"Yes, of course."

"Mummy doesn't let me open presents on Christmas Eve," she said as she stared down at the package with the plaid bow.

"Well, this can be our little secret." Hilde pulled up a plush stool and perched on the edge of it.

Marigold giggled and pulled open the ribbon, then shoved aside the paper. The lovely scarf shimmered in the soft light of the room. She hadn't imagined it then. The material really did have a luster to it.

The girl stared at it for a long moment. It occurred to Hilde that the scarf was a much too grown-up gift for her. Perhaps she should have gotten her a plush toy instead. But she pulled it out of the wrapping and held it up, then cradled the soft material against her cheek with a smile.

"It's soft," she said.

"Let me help you."

Hilde took the scarf and wrapped it around her neck in a stylized fashion making the young girl appear far more older and sophisticated than she actually was. In her mind's eye, she had a vision of the girl grown and just as beautiful as ever.

"There, now," Hilde said.

"Thank you, auntie." She granted her a smile and sounded grown up.

Hilde always thought she was wise beyond her years. She was somewhat of an old soul, so the gift of the scarf appeared to be appropriate for her.

"Are you going to tell me a story, auntie?"

And then just like that, she sounded like a little girl again.

Hilde grinned. "Of course, I am."

Marigold sat up straighter in the bed, her eyes alight with joyful anticipation. "What story will this be? One about Christmas?"

"Even better. One about Christmas and a pair of magical shoes."

Before she started, her sister came in with a cup of steaming tea for her and hot cocoa for Marigold. She kissed her daughter on the head.

"Aunt Hilde brought me this gift!"

"I see." She fingered the soft material. "It's lovely," and then to her sister, "and so grown up. She's only six. And I thought we agreed no presents on Christmas Eve."

Hilde merely shrugged. She sipped her tea, giving Marigold a wink over the rim.

"Don't stay up too late if you want Santa to come."

"I know you and Papa are Santa, Mummy."

Her sister's eyebrows raised in question.

"I didn't tell her," Hilde said.

"I've always known, Mummy," the girl said.

"We'll see in the morning, won't we?" Her sister turned to her then. "Not too late, Hilde."

She waved away her sister as she left the room and closed the door behind her. "Now, let's see. Where was I?"

"A Christmas story about a pair of magical shoes!" Marigold reminded her and bounced in the bed.

"Ah, yes. Once upon a time, there was a beautiful young girl. She lived with her stepmother and stepsisters, but they weren't nice to her. She worked as a servant in her own home."

Marigold gasped and shook her head. "That's so mean."

"Yes, but then one day, a pair of shoes changed her life..."

Chapter 1

The chiming of the clock tower in Whitebridge clanged the early morning hour. It was a faint *bong, bong, bong* that Ella counted as she laid awake in her narrow, lumpy bed under the thin blanket dreading the coming day. Dread was part of her morning routine now.

Sunlight peeked through the shabby draperies at her window as dawn arrived. Even as another day of labor loomed, nothing killed the spirit of the season inside her. Not even her stepmother and stepsisters. Not even their nasty dispositions or the fact that her stepmother, Lillian, refused to decorate for Christmas.

Except for a sad looking tree in the foyer with a few decorations.

But Ella was not to be dissuaded. She dragged out all her mother's favorite decorations and placed them around her shabby third-floor bedroom, trying to make the drab appearance a bit more cheerful. She placed her favorite decoration on the top of the tree—a beautiful gold star.

She loved Christmas.

She shoved the blanket aside and walked to the window, pushing open the curtain to peer down at the estate that had fallen into disrepair. Since her father's disappearance on a merchant trip several years ago, Lillian squandered what was left of the estate's money on satin and lace, shoes and parasols for her two spoiled daughters. Meanwhile, the small manor they lived in needed many repairs.

In the distance, the offending clock tower stood tall and proud and ruled her day. From her window, the peak of it was clear as well as the high turrets and heraldry of Whitebridge Palace. What was it like living in a castle? Would she be a maid as she was here? Or would she find herself as one of the noble ladies wearing beautiful gowns and having her every whim attended?

She sighed when the rooster crowed. It was time to start the day. She looked out as the sun peeked over the horizon, illuminating the outline of the castle beyond and the dusting of snow on the cold ground.

"One day, Papa," she whispered, "I will find my way out of here."

She often spoke to her father, even though he'd been gone all these long years.

She dressed, tied her long dark hair back with a blue ribbon, and headed down to the kitchen for the day. She put a tea kettle on to boil. Outside, she fed the chickens and gathered eggs, petted the dog, and gave the cat his breakfast. In the distance, at the pond, geese honked their arrival. She smiled. Later she would walk out to the edge of the pond and feed them, too.

The servant's bell rang. Her stepmother. She poured hot water into the tea kettle, made a breakfast of porridge, eggs, and toast, and then carried it up to the woman's room. At the top of the stairs, she turned right and headed down the hall to the largest bedroom. She rapped twice and waited.

"Enter," came the abrupt, muffled response.

Ella pushed open the door. Just as she did, the cat sprinted past her and hopped onto the oversized bed where her stepmother sat waiting for her breakfast. The woman's salt-and-pepper hair was tucked under her nightcap. Crinkles were at the corners of each eye and her mouth was drawn down into a permanent grimace. No doubt due to being unhappy for so many years. Her thin lips were a deep red, high severe cheekbones and a chin that ended in a point. She petted the cat, her long slender fingers ruffling the fur between his shoulders. Loud purrs emanated from the small feline.

"Good morning, Stepmother," she greeted in her best pleasant voice.

"Where is my newspaper?" her stepmother asked.

"I'll fetch it for you." Ella placed the tray with the breakfast on the woman's lap. She did a quick curtsy then dashed from the room.

She hurried down the stairs to the front door and pulled it open. The rolled-up paper was on the doorstep as usual. But even so, Ella saw the hint of the headline. Something about a royal decree. As she snatched it off the stoop, she heard Lucinda shouting her name.

"*Ella!* Where is my breakfast?"

Ella hurried back up the stairs to her stepmother's room, her chest heaving a bit and her legs burning from her brief sprint. Jet had curled up next to her in the bed, eyeing the breakfast tray.

"Your newspaper, stepmother."

She scowled as she snatched it from Ella's hands, then opened it with a snap. She glowered at her over the edge of the paper.

"What are you gawking at, girl? Don't you have chores?"

Another quick curtsy. "Yes, Stepmother."

"*ELLA!*" Lucinda shouted again.

Ella hurried back down the stairs to the kitchen. As she arrived, the other two bells were ringing. One for Lucinda and one for Daniella. She quickly made their breakfast trays. It was a balancing act, but she managed to carry both at the same time back up the stairs. By the time she arrived at the landing, her legs were burning and her arms ached. She used her elbow to push open the door to Lucinda's room.

"There you are! You lazy thing."

Lucinda might have been pretty if not for her ugly personality. She had unruly red hair, bright blue eyes, a bulbous nose, which Ella assumed she got from her father, a square chin, and a face rather like a horse. She was tall and lanky and flat chested. Her taste in gowns was ostentatious in bright, horrid colors. And while her stepmother gave her singing lessons, the girl couldn't carry a tune for anything.

"Good morning, Lucinda."

"About time you came. I was about to waste away to nothing!"

Ella resisted the urge to roll her eyes as she placed the serving tray on Lucinda's lap. She hurried out of the room to avoid any more chastising. At Daniella's room, she knocked once and then pushed open the door. Daniella was unlike her sister. Her black hair was long, her eyes the color of coal. She had a long, thin nose much like her mother's that gave her a pinched expression and a nasal sound to her voice. She was plump around the middle and short. Her taste in clothes was somewhat subdued compared to her sister, but she still favored bright colors in loud patterns.

"Good morning, Daniella."

"You're late," the girl snapped. "And why does Lucinda always get her breakfast first? It's not fair."

As the youngest, Daniella often felt as though she was slighted. Ella said nothing as she placed the tray on the girl's lap and then scurried out of the room.

"You didn't open my drapes!" Daniella shouted.

Ella halted and immediately returned to the room. She pushed aside the heavy velvet draperies on the one window, letting the morning sun into the shadowy confines of the room. When she shoved open the drapes, dust motes danced in the slashes of sunlight.

"When are you going to clean my drapes?" the girl complained and then sneezed. "See what it does to me?"

"Tomorrow, Daniella."

"I think you should do it *today*."

But today was market day. "I will try."

"If you don't do it, I'll tell my mother!" It was always her go-to threat.

"Yes, Daniella."

Ella understood that was the only correct response when it came to those threats. She nodded and hurried out of the room before she was assigned more chores that weren't on her list today.

She scurried back down to the kitchen. Once there, she put on her walking shoes, threw her threadbare shawl around her shoulders and tied a kerchief over her hair. She snatched up the small basket she used for vegetables and fruit, but when she headed for the backdoor, her stepmother rang the servant's bell again. It was a never-ending cycle with them.

Ella removed the shawl and the kerchief and placed the basket on the counter. She returned to her stepmother's room to collect her empty breakfast dishes.

"Ella, the paper says there's a royal decree."

She tapped the news print with her index finger, the blue jeweled ring glittering in the early morning light. Mischievous excitement crossed her stepmother's features.

"There's to be a royal Christmas ball in one week's time in which the prince will select his bride from all the eligible maidens of the kingdom. All are invited!"

"A ball?" Ella gasped.

"Yes, a ball, you dolt," she snapped. "We must see what appropriate gowns the girls have to wear. If we need to have dresses made, I will need to go to town this afternoon." She paused and gave Ella a glare with her beady blue eyes. "Well? Why are you standing there?" She snapped her fingers. "Get to it!"

"You said all eligible maidens," she said. "Does that mean I can go, too?"

"You?" she said and laughed. Then she tapped her chin with her forefinger. "Yes, I suppose it does."

Elation skipped through her. She had never been to a ball before. She hoped she had something to wear. Perhaps something of her mother's even if it was a tad out of fashion.

"Oh, thank you, Stepmother. Thank—"

"But..." She said, interrupting her momentary joy. "All your chores must be finished by then *including* helping with the gowns for the girls. The mending, the sewing, the cleaning, the cooking. All of it."

Her heart sank, but still a tiny bit of hope glimmered deep down. Perhaps she would be able to get it all done in time for the ball.

"Yes, Stepmother. Of course."

"Now, be gone." She waved her away with the swish of a hand.

As Ella headed for the door, Lucinda and Daniella rushed in, their eyes alight with excitement.

"Mother! Did I hear you say there was to be a royal ball?" Lucinda said.

Ella had no doubt Lucinda eavesdropped on their conversation and then brought Daniella along with her to gossip about the upcoming ball with their mother. As she made her way down the stairs, her heart sank lower and lower and she understood she would not be going to the market today or the ball.

Chapter 2

Ella dashed between Lucinda's room and Daniella's room gathering accessories and gowns and then helping each of them try everything on. All the while, her stepmother hovered behind her telling her what to put on and what to take off.

She helped Lucinda into a bright pink gown with a full skirt. The neckline was trimmed in orange roses. The colors clashed with her red hair. It was absolutely hideous but Ella managed to keep her face expressionless.

"No, no, no!" her stepmother said and then gave an exasperated sigh. "This is not befitting a royal ball. Take that off at once." She snapped her fingers.

"But, Mother, I like this one!" Lucinda whined. She twirled to show off the full skirt which was devoid of petticoats.

"Not that one. Ella, get her out of it. Where is Daniella?"

"Here, Mother."

Ella began to undo all the tiny buttons down the back of Lucinda's gown as Daniella trotted in wearing a blue gown that had seen better days and was definitely out of fashion. It had a scooped neckline and a dropped narrow waist that flowed into a full skirt.

The skirt was adorned with ribbons and bows and pink rosettes in the knot of each bow. Unlike her sister, Daniella insisted on the petticoats. She happily twirled with a squeal to show off the fullness.

Stepmother's face contorted into one of horror. It took everything inside Ella not to giggle.

Her stepmother clucked her tongue in disgust. "That simply won't do either. I must go to the dressmaker to order new gowns before he's too busy to take new orders."

Ella also needed to go to market and hesitated to ask. She hated the thought of traveling with that woman, but there were things she needed for the kitchen.

"Pardon me, Stepmother, may I accompany you? I have a market order to pick up."

She looked down her nose at Ella with reproach. "Yes, I suppose you can. But ask for nothing at the dressmaker."

"Yes, of course." She gave a nod of understanding.

"Oh, can I come, too?" Lucinda asked with a catty smile. She gave Ella a cutting look, clearly not wanting to be outdone.

Ella cringed. The last thing she wanted was to have to go to the village with both her stepmother and Lucinda.

"Me, too!" cried Daniella.

Ella frowned.

"Does that not suit you, Ella?" her stepmother snapped. Her face contorted into an evil scowl.

As much as she tried to be careful with her facial expressions, she couldn't keep it to herself this time.

"It suits fine, Stepmother," she replied and gave a cheerful smile.

But her stepmother continued to glower at her. Ella ignored her as she hurried down the stairs to the kitchen to cover her hair with her kerchief, wrap the thin shawl around her shoulders, and grab her basket. She heard the commotion of the three of them heading down the stairs to the front door. Ella hurried to catch up to them knowing her stepmother wouldn't wait for her. As she came through the hall, they were at the door. Both Lucinda and Daniella peered at her with disgust.

"Does she *have* to travel with us? I mean, look at her." Lucinda waved a hand at her.

Ella stood her ground, refusing to be intimidated by her. She was aware of the shabby state of her dress and the shoes that were nearly worn through.

"We don't want to be seen with a *servant*," Daniella added.

"Girls, please. We will take the carriage. Ella can walk."

And that was that. The girls giggled with delight as they scampered out the door and to the one carriage they had. Her only consolation was that at least it wasn't an enclosed carriage and they would have to deal with the morning sunlight on their faces as they headed to the market.

She waited for them to get down the road a bit before she started her journey to the market. She much preferred to walk alone anyway. They were nothing but hateful shrews and she didn't want to listen to their barbs the entire ride there and back.

The market was its usual bustle of activity. Decorations for the upcoming season were throughout the small village. Garland decorated with colorful lights was strung across the street from one building to the next. Festive wreaths with ribbons were on every shop door. There was a sense of cheerfulness about the village people and shopkeepers. It was infectious. Ella couldn't help but smile as she strolled through the streets, greeting people with a smile and a nod.

She loved Christmas. It was her favorite time of year. Well, it used to be when her mother was alive. She was unable to enjoy it as she used to with her stepmother and stepsisters in the house. They made her life a living hell as she served them day and night, never getting a day off. Not even Christmas or the day after. Still, she found a way to celebrate in her own quiet way. She hoarded a few treats for herself to enjoy long after they went to bed on Christmas Day.

Young women everywhere were in a fit of excitement over the announcement of the upcoming ball. She wished she was able to share in their excitement, but she knew there was no way her stepmother would allow her to attend. She was a servant girl, after all.

At the general store, she headed to the counter to pick up her order of eggs, bread, sugar and tea. The proprietor was a nice man by the name of Mr. Gibson. She gave him her best smile.

"Good morning, Mr. Gibson."

"Ah, Ella. Here to pick up your order?"

"Yes, thank you."

His brows drew together in a look of regret. "I hate to ask, Ella, but do you have the money to pay the balance on your account first?"

"My stepmother pays that weekly."

"Ah..." He scratched his balding head. "I'm afraid she hasn't in weeks."

"Weeks?" Ella's heart picked up. "What do you mean, weeks?"

"It's just that the account has a bit of a balance and, well, I can't be letting you have your order without payment."

"How much is owed?" she asked.

"A hundred pounds." His shoulders slumped as he said it, a mixture of sadness and hesitation evident in his voice.

Ella swallowed hard as mortification swept through her. How could her stepmother not pay the bill? What was she doing with the household money?

"I'm sorry, Ella."

She didn't know what to do. She needed those items for the rest of the week. If she didn't have them, then how was she to make the tea they expected for breakfast every day? She bit her lip as she made a decision that would likely get her into more trouble than she'd ever been in.

"If I promise to pay you in full by the end of the week, may I have my order?"

Mr. Gibson glanced around the store to see if anyone else was within earshot. Luckily, there wasn't.

"I shouldn't..." he said.

Ella leaned across the counter and whispered, "Please, sir."

He shifted from one foot to the other as he ran a hand over his shiny pate. "If you promise?"

"I do."

He turned from the counter, went into the back and returned a moment later with her items. She took them, grateful he gave them to her and then dashed from the shop before he changed his mind.

How was she going to get a hundred pounds? As she walked down the street, her basket full of goods on her arm, she spied her stepsisters and stepmother coming out the dressmaker's shop. Both Lucinda and Daniella wore grins, their faces lit with excitement, as they skipped along the street talking about how much they were going to love their new gowns. And one for her stepmother, of course. Nothing for Ella. It wasn't even a thought.

She watched them for a moment, reminding herself to be kind as all sorts of horrid thoughts came into her mind. She didn't want to wish ill on anyone, but she hoped Lucinda ended up with a giant pus-filled blemish on the day of the ball. And maybe Daniella would burn her hair when she tried to curl it.

Ella reprimanded herself for her mean thoughts. She was about to step into the street to cross, when a red and gold coach rumbled down the street. It was absolutely ornate with gold trimmings, a footman, a driver, and four white chargers. Ella's breath caught in her throat as it came to a halt not far from where she stood.

A tall, beautiful woman stepped out with the help of her footman. She wore a magnificent red velvet gown and a matching cloak trimmed in ermine. Her silvery hair was piled high on her head in the latest fashion. Dainty curls framed her face. She had bright blue eyes and lips the color of the red rose. Even her cheeks were rosy. She noticed Ella gaping at her and gave her a bright smile.

"Good morrow, young miss."

"H-hello."

"Why, aren't you a pretty thing." Her smile was infectious.

Ella glanced down to her worn shoes. "Thank you, but I'm not."

"Nonsense!"

The woman approached her, looking her up and down with curiosity. When Ella failed to lift her gaze to hers, the woman put a finger under her chin and tipped it up with a gentle nudge.

"I can see into the depths of your deep brown eyes," the woman said. "I see a lot of heartache."

Ella's stomach twisted into a knot.

"But there is also kindness," she continued. "What's your name, dearest?"

"Ella," she said, her voice quiet.

"Ah, a beautiful name to match the girl! Wouldn't you agree, Percy?" she said to the footman.

"Yes, madam," the footman replied in a monotone. He never cast a glance toward Ella.

The woman latched her arm around Ella's. "Dear Percy. He always agrees with me. It's why I keep him around."

She laughed, her eyes twinkling with a sort of mirth Ella had never seen before. She liked her right away.

"Now, tell me, dearest Ella. What are you planning to wear to the ball?"

Ella blinked in confusion. Had the woman not seen her ragged dress, her thin shawl, her worn out shoes?

"I-I'm not going."

"Not going!" She clucked her tongue. "Why not?"

"I don't have anything suitable to wear, madam."

"Madam!" She said on a gasp and then a laugh. "You must call me Noella."

"Oh, but I—"

"I *insist*. Now, what do you say we pop on over to the dressmaker and order you something exquisite for the ball? I personally know him and he's sure to give me exactly what I want."

Panic rose in Ella. She tugged her arm away from the woman's. "Thank you, but I can't accept."

She stuck out her bottom lip in an exaggerated pout. "Why not?"

Ella started to back away from the woman. "It's generous, to be sure, but I don't know you and, well, my father said never to accept gifts from strangers."

"Your father said that, hm?" She tapped her finger on her chin as she gave Percy a glance.

He slowly shook his head. "Madam, it appears she doesn't know who you are."

"Yes, it would seem that way." She turned back to Ella, who had put considerable distance between them as she backed away. "My dear, I'm Noella Fairchild. Have you never heard that name before?"

"No." She shook her head. "I do thank you for thinking of me, madam, but I simply must go."

Before Noella Fairchild said another word, Ella spun and dashed up the street. She didn't stop running until she was at the end of the market on the dirt road heading back to home.

Noella Fairchild watched the young girl hurry down the path and disappear, her tattered skirts fluttering around her ankles. Using her magic, she sensed a sort of sadness mixed with a deep hope of better days to come. Well, she could give her that.

"Percy, follow her. Find out where she lives and report back."

Percy nodded. "Yes, madam."

Her long-time servant followed the girl's path. Percy understood discretion better than anyone. She'd know everything there was to know about the girl by the time he returned in a few hours. Smiling, she returned to the carriage to await news of the girl.

CHAPTER 3

By the time Ella reached home, she was out of breath. Her legs burned from the sprint from the market. She had no idea who Noella Fairchild was. She'd been a resident of the village since she was born and had never heard the name.

Then again, she only ventured to the market once a week and then it was a quick trip there and back. She had so much work to do. She hung up her shawl and kerchief and paused a moment in the kitchen to catch her breath. But as she did so, the three women rang for her. It was time for luncheon and she hadn't anything prepared.

She had several slices of bread leftover from the previous day and quickly put them in a linen lined bowl and covered them. That would have to do for the time being. Swallowing hard, she headed to the dining room to face her stepmother and tell her it would be at least another hour before luncheon was served.

Her stepmother sat at the head of the table. She placed the bowl in the middle. Her stepmother shoved off the linen cover and glowered at the bread. Her fiery glare bored into Ella with a searing intensity. Her anger radiated from her like waves of blistering heat.

"Stale bread is all you have to offer for luncheon?"

"I've only just returned from the market and—"

"I don't want your excuses," she snapped.

Ella stood frozen in place, the words clotting her throat.

"Well, get to it!" she said.

She hurried out of the dining room as Lucinda and Daniella snickered. In the kitchen, Ella put together their luncheon including a small portion for herself. After she served them, she returned to the kitchen where she sat alone at the scarred wooden table and stared down at her half-empty plate.

A knock on the back door startled her.

She opened the door to see an elderly man standing on the other side. He was hunched over and held a gnarled cane in one hand. The knit cap on his head barely covered his ears. His jacket was threadbare with what appeared to be a moth-eaten hole on his shoulder. When he smiled, he had crooked stump teeth, his face wrinkling with the movement making his eyes squint.

"Beggin' ya pardon, miss. I was walking down the road there heading through town to the next." He pointed to the road behind the house. "Could ya spare a wee bit of bread and water for me?"

Ella hesitated.

"I don't want to be any trouble. Just a bit a bread and then I'll be on me way, eh?"

"Just a moment." She pushed the door closed.

She found two-day old bread which she cut in half and wrapped into a linen napkin for him. She poured water in a small cup, then reopened the door. She handed him the bread.

"This is all I have."

"Thank ya, miss." He took the bread and cradled it against his chest as if it were a prize.

"And water." She handed him the cup.

He drained it, then returned it to her with a smile of thanks. "I'll be on me way, now. Thank ya, miss."

She watched him hobble away back toward the road before she closed the door. It was odd, really. There were rarely strangers in the area and certainly they didn't knock on doors and ask for food and water. It occurred to her, too, how strange it was she'd met two strangers in one day.

But she paid it no more mind as she set about cleaning the kitchen of the luncheon dishes and prepared for dinner that evening, humming a familiar Christmas tune her mother used to sing to her. It gave her comfort as she went through the day's drudgery.

Noella Fairchild waited for Percy's return in the carriage at the edge of the village on the dirt road. She shivered even under her thick cloak as the wind turned from the north. With a flick of her wrist, an ermine-lined muff appeared in a sprinkling of fairy dust on her hands. She settled back into the seat to wait.

She dozed off, her head against the padded wall, as the sun dipped to the horizon. Percy had been gone for quite some time. No doubt doing all he could to find out who the girl was.

"Here he comes now, madam," the driver called.

Noella jarred awake at the driver's words. She pushed open the carriage door and hopped out, eager to hear the results of her footman's investigation.

Percy was more than a footman, though. He'd been with her for more years than she counted as her advisor in all matters. Even when she came up with the foolish idea of finding a suitable young woman for her son. He'd tried to talk her out of it, but she had refused to listen.

"Well?" she asked as soon as Percy was within earshot. "What did you find out?"

"She lives in a small house a few miles that way with her stepmother and stepsisters." He pointed back up the road behind him. "She's a servant, madam. The three women she lives with are less than kind to her." He sniffed derision.

"A servant girl, you say." She tapped her finger against her chin.

"However," he continued as if she hadn't spoken. "She is kind despite being treated as though she were nothing more than dirt on their shoes. She gave me stale bread." He held up the bundle.

Noella's eyes widened in shock as her heart did a quick *thunk*. "She didn't recognize you, did she?"

"No, madam. My disguise was convincing."

Noella nodded. "Good, good. Do you think she's worthy?"

He tilted his head to the side making a curl of dark hair fall across his broad forehead. "Madam, I believe only you have the answer to that. I will say, though, she was singing a familiar Christmas tune as I left."

Her heart swelled with joyous anticipation. Excitement skittered through her as her mind raced with possibilities. She swung open the carriage door with alacrity.

"That's good to hear, Percy. Come! We have much work to do!"

Percy climbed in after her and closed the door.

"Let's away, Alfred!"

The carriage lurched forward as the horses started a swift gallop.

"I do hope you know what you're doing, madam."

"I do, too, Percy. I do, too."

CHAPTER 4

The day of the Christmas ball arrived. Ella had returned to the dressmaker's shop in the market to pick up the three gowns for Lillian, Daniella, and Lucinda. As she helped them dress, she thought of the woman she met the day she went to the grocery. She wondered, not for the first time, who Noella Fairchild was and why she had offered to give her a gown for the ball.

Ella waited for them at the foot of the stairs. Lucinda descended first in a bright yellow gown trimmed with the ruffles around the scooped neckline and the full skirt. She flashed Ella a wicked smile. Daniella was right behind her wearing a turquoise gown in the same style with the same ruffle around the scooped neckline. Each of them had fur-lined cloaks to match their gowns. With their bright and flamboyant colors, Ella decided both of them would be quite out of place at an elegant Christmas ball.

Lillian was the next to descend the stairs, pulling on her black satin upper length gloves. At least she had the good sense to wear something in subdued colors as befitting a widow of her age and station. Her gown was a dark emerald green with a slim waist and a narrow skirt.

"We're off to the ball," her stepmother announced as the two girls exited the house. "While we're gone, I expect the floors to be scrubbed, the draperies and tapestries cleaned, and the silver polished to a high shine. One of my girls will no doubt return with the prince's favor." She cackled as she left the house, slamming the door behind her, not even waiting for a response from Ella.

"Yes, Stepmother," she whispered under her breath.

Tears blurred her eyes, her heart aching, as she sprinted up the stairs to the third floor. She flung herself on her narrow bed, burying her face into the pillow and weeping. She had so wanted to go. Regret swept through her. She should have accepted the mysterious woman's offer of a gown. But then, how would she explain that to her stepmother?

She hadn't been able to get the one hundred pounds for Mr. Gibson, either. When she went searching for the ledger book her father had once kept in the oak desk in the study, she couldn't find it. All she found was an empty leather money purse. All of the household funds had been squandered on the new gowns.

When she finished crying, she sat back on the bed and stared at the curtains hanging at her grimy window. A pale slash of moonlight came through, leaving a blue-white glow on the wood flooring. She wiped her tears and walked to the window, pushing aside one of the panels and peering out at the lawn below. Snow fell, leaving a dusting on the ground below.

As she stared out the window, she thought she saw the flash of a shadowy shape through the front yard to her left. Her heart kicked into a wild beat. Was someone out there? Another shadowy shape then went through the yard back the way it had come. She sucked in a sharp breath.

What was that?

She spun from the window, looking for a weapon. All she came up with was a hairbrush. She snatched it off the bureau and crept to the door, her heart in her throat as she paused to listen. There was nothing but silence.

Her slippers were silent on the stairs as she made her way down. She paused at the front door, pressing an ear against it. She heard nothing.

A swift knock on the kitchen door startled her. She jumped, a breath of a gasp escaping as she stared into the shadows of the house wishing she had thought to light a few candles before she dashed upstairs to feel sorry for herself.

Her hands shaking, she made her way from the front door to the kitchen. Her breath hitched as she paused there to listen.

More silence.

In the kitchen, she traded the hairbrush for a broom and crept to the back door. Her hand paused at the knob, wondering if she should open it. Her heart was in her throat as she twisted the knob and then flung open the door. She shoved the broom handle in front of her as a weapon.

But there was no one there.

Snowflakes drifted from the night sky in a silent dance. She stepped in the threshold and leaned out, looking left and right. Nothing.

As she turned to go inside, something on the doorstep caught her eye. It was a small green box with a red ribbon wrapped around it and a giant red bow on top. She leaned the broom against the door jamb and knelt.

A nametag stuck out from under the ribbon. *TO ELLA* was written in big, perfect letters.

Her brows drew together as she stood once more, glancing around again. There were no footprints in the dusting of snow or the mud to indicate someone had been there to drop it off. She was certain she had heard the distinct knock on the back door, though.

She bent to pick up the box, then kicked the door closed with her heel as she placed it on the kitchen table. Before she opened it, she lit a candle to give her some light. Then she stared at it as if it were a foreign object.

Who sent it?

With a shaking hand, she tugged on the bow. The silken ribbon slipped away with ease and fell away. She pulled off the lid and set it aside. White tissue paper covered whatever was inside.

Her heart pounded hard as she pushed aside the tissue to reveal another note written in the same handwriting as the nametag. It read, *PUT THESE ON.*

She picked up the note, wondering who sent it and why. Below the note was the most dazzling pair of shoes she had ever seen. She picked up one of the shoes and realized with a gasp it was made of glass. The candlelight glinted off the surface, making a rainbow of prisms reflect on the old wood table.

"Glass slippers," she whispered.

She glanced back down at the note telling her to put them on. Would they fit? How did this person who left them know they would fit?

There was only one way to find out.

She slipped her feet out of her worn shoes and placed both glass slippers on the floor in front of her. She stared down at them, her heart ramming hard in her chest from both anticipation and apprehension. Taking a deep breath, she slipped first one foot and then the other into the shoes.

They were magnificent. And despite being made of glass, the footbed was cushiony. She pulled back her tattered skirt and stared down at them. They were the most beautiful shoes she had ever worn. They had a rounded toe and a one-inch heel to make it easy for her to walk in them.

As she peered down at them, something began to happen. It was as though the room spun around her, starting off slow and then going faster and faster and faster. She pressed a hand against her head as a dizziness came upon her and she suddenly felt as though she might faint. She stumbled, trying to maintain her footing but she couldn't.

Everything spun out of control. A cool breeze went through her hair as it lifted from her neck. Her tattered servant's dress morphed and changed into something else. She didn't quite understand what was happening or why.

Then the world came to a halt and she found herself standing outside the gates of the palace.

She took a step back, shocked and wondering how she ended up there when she didn't take one step outside of the house.

As she looked down at her gown, she realized she was dressed in the most beautiful red ball gown. She swished the full skirt from side to side, watching as it sparkled in the half light. Roses the same color as the gown dotted the skirt and around the waist. The long sheer sleeves came to a point on her hands. The bodice was covered in sparkles and more roses. She stuck out a foot from under the miles of petticoats to see the glass slippers still on her feet. She patted her hair to find it was coiled on top of her head in the fashion of the day.

All of this was so strange. And wonderful.

"There you are!"

The exclamation made her jump. Noella Fairchild bustled from the shadows and took her by the arm, leading her through the gates of the palace.

"My dear, you are radiant."

"I don't understand. How—"

"Nothing to understand," she said with an encouraging, infectious smile. "We must get you to the ball quickly."

"But, madam—"

"You *must* call me Noella." She flashed a grin.

Ella pulled her to a stop. "I don't understand any of this. Who *are* you?"

"Why, I'm your fairy godmother, dear. Now come, come, come. You don't want to miss another minute." She took her by the arm and hurried toward the stairs at the palace entrance once again.

"My fairy godmother?"

"Yes, of course. Now, remember, you *must* remove the shoes before the last stroke of midnight," she said.

"What happens then?"

"Why, the spell will be broken, of course. Ah, here we are!"

They arrived at the palace doors and halted.

"Here's where I leave you, my dear." She stepped back, her face winsome. "You're positively stunning. You're sure to turn the head of my s—er, the prince." She shooed her toward the steps. "Go on!"

Ella hesitated a moment before beginning the ascent to the palace entrance. Then she turned back and hugged Noella.

"Thank you," she whispered.

The woman was so taken aback by the gesture, she didn't immediately return the hug. When she did, it was warm and wonderful and reminded Ella of her mother who she had lost when she was a little girl. Noella patted her back, then gave her one last squeeze before releasing her and stepping back. She gave her an encouraging nod.

Taking a deep breath, Ella picked up her skirts and ascended the steps.

CHAPTER 5

E lla made her way to the top of the palace steps and entered. With wide-eyed wonder, she followed the line of guards to the grand ballroom. As she passed through one hallway, she caught a glimpse of herself in the reflection of a tall mirror and stopped. She gawkcd at the unfamiliar image, then stepped a little closer.

Not only was her dark hair coiled on top of her head, but it sparkled. Velvet red ribbon weaved through the locks ending at the nape of her neck in a lovely little bow. Coiled strands framed her face that no longer looked as though she was tired. The dark circles under her eyes were even gone. And the gown...

She giggled as she spun, letting the layers of the skirt fly around her. It was the most beautiful gown she had ever seen with the applique roses around the bodice, the waist, and down the skirt. She pressed her fingers against her lips. She felt like a fairy princess.

The sound of music spurred her into action. She hurried away from the mirror. Noella was right—she didn't want to miss another minute.

The guards opened the doors for her as she approached. She gave them both a smile and a nod as she passed through and headed down the stairs, taking them slowly one at a time, her feet silent on the plush garnet rug. Both sides of the banisters were covered in lighted green garland. Flanking the bottom of the stairs were two enormous green trees decorated with red and gold Christmas balls and white twinkle lights.

Lighted swags of garland hung from the rafters of the ceiling. On one end of the massive ballroom, a giant tree decorated with lights. Next to the tree, the king sat in an opulent chair on a raised dais overseeing the events. Standing next to him was the prince wearing a white double-breasted jacket, white trousers and knee-high black boots polished to a high shine. On the other end, the orchestra played a lovely waltz. The dance floor was crowded with couples in their finery while other spectators stood at the edge of the dance floor.

Everything about it was magical and it made her smile as she took the last step off the stairs and entered the room. Heads turned as she made her way through the ballroom, her eyes alight with wonder at everything and everyone.

The waltz ended. The couples on the dance floor stopped moving, clapped, and then moved to the edge of the room. It was the prince, then, who walked from the king's side to the center of the ballroom. Ella paused, observing his seamless movements with graceful finesse, his attention sweeping across all the ladies in the room. Her heart leapt to her throat as he lingered on her for a long moment, his focus intense. Then he stepped toward her, his intensity growing as he halted and then lifted his hand...to the woman standing next to her.

He bowed his head to her. "My lady, will you do me the honor?"

Ella's heart sank as the woman dressed in a stunning sapphire gown took his hand. Together, the stepped into the center of the ballroom. The music started and they began to dance.

She thought for sure he was going to ask her to dance. She turned away, deciding that being here, at the Christmas ball was enough for her. Especially when she thought she wouldn't be able to attend at all.

Across the ballroom, she spied her stepmother standing behind Lucinda and Daniella. She gave them both a nudge to dance with other suitors. They were hard to miss in their vibrant colored dresses. She spun away to avoid them, hoping they hadn't seen her. As she did, she crashed right into the chest of a tall man. He gripped her upper arms to keep her from losing her balance in the glass slippers.

"Whoa there, my lady. Are you all right?"

She tipped her head up to look into the most dazzling blue eyes she had ever seen. He was handsome with thick, wavy chestnut hair that was long enough to touch his collar. There was an inherent, rugged strength about his face with a strong jaw, high cheekbones, a firm mouth. Touches of humor were around his mouth and at the corners of his eyes. He wore a deep blue double-breasted jacket with gold buttons and a spray of holly in the lapel. The long sleeves had turned back cuffs, also with gold buttons, and an elaborate gold trim around the top of the cuff. His white trousers were pristine, a stark contrast to his tall black boots. His cravat was the same color as his trousers, giving him an elegant and distinguished appearance.

"I'm terribly sorry. I didn't mean to—" She clamped her mouth closed with a snap.

"Are you hurt?" he asked, looking her over with concern.

She shook her head as he released her arms. Then she did a quick curtsy.

"My apologies, my lord."

He laughed. "I am no lord." He held his white-gloved hand out to her. "Care to dance?"

"I..." She cut a glance through the crowd, but didn't see her stepsisters anywhere. She turned back to him, looking up into those incredible, mesmerizing eyes. What harm would one dance do? "Yes, I would."

She placed her hand in his and he led her to the dance floor. He placed his free hand on her waist. She put her hand on his shoulder as he spun her to the music, falling into place with the other couples in a seamless fashion that felt completely right.

"What's your name?" he asked.

She focused on his perfect cravat, the way it knotted at his throat with the tiny gold pin. "Ella," she said.

"Pleased to meet you, Ella. I'm Nicholas."

He twirled her about the dance floor with ease and sure-footed expertise. She was exhilarated to be in his arms, to sway along with the intoxicating music. She continued to fix her attention on the pin at his throat and realized it was a tiny gold star with what appeared to be a diamond in the center.

"Nicholas not a lord?" She tipped her head up and gave him a playful smile.

He laughed, a deep rumble in his throat. "Indeed, no."

"Well, I'm no lady."

"Are you not? That's rather refreshing to hear," he said.

"Is it? Why is that?"

He twirled her, then brought her close, his hand firmly planted on her waist. "I grow tired of pompous ladies who think they are better than anyone."

As he said it, he glanced around the room, his eyes landing on one particular lady. As they turned, Ella followed his gaze to a striking young woman who was tall, with pale features, red lips, high cheekbones, black hair hanging in waves about her face, which was not the fashion of the court. She wore a lovely navy satin gown overlaid with delicate gold lace. She held a fan to her face, hiding behind it as her eyes tracked Nicholas's every move. Ella didn't miss the penetrating stare she gave her as they twirled.

"You dance beautifully," he said, trying to make small talk.

"Thank you. My father taught me."

She glanced up at him through her lashes. He was smiling down at her, sending a warmth through her she had never experienced before.

"I should like to meet your father someday." He winked.

She flinched.

His smile and smirk faded. "I'm sorry. Did I say something wrong?"

"My father is no longer with me," she said, returning her attention to the star pin.

"My apologies, my lady."

"He's been gone for several years," she said. "I miss him a lot. I don't know why I'm telling you this."

Her spun her one last time as the music ended. His hand remained on her waist. Her hand on his shoulder as she glanced up at him, reluctant to release him. Though, she thought, he seemed reluctant to release her as well. Another waltz started.

His attention briefly flickered to someone behind her.

Without asking, he whisked her back onto the dance floor. Ella had the distinct feeling he was trying to dodge the young woman in the navy and gold gown.

"Are you avoiding someone?" she asked, one brow raised high as she looked up at him.

He swallowed so hard, his throat worked up and down. "Would you think ill of me if I was?"

"I should say not. I hardly know you," she said.

He pulled her into a tighter embrace, his voice dangerously low as he spoke. "Yes, I am avoiding someone. She's been trying to dance with me all night. The lovely and mysterious Lady Eloise Winterbourne."

"Why are you avoiding her?" Ella asked, genuinely curious.

"I'm afraid I don't fancy her as much as she fancies me," he said.

"And so, you picked me to dance with instead?"

"No, my dear, you ran into me and gave me no choice."

He gave her a sly wink that sent a warm shiver through her down to her toes.

"I hope you don't mind if I take all the dances on your dance card," he said.

"I have no dance card," she replied.

"Then it's settled! You'll be my partner for the rest of the evening."

"Much to the dismay of the Lady Eloise," Ella said, flashing a wicked grin.

The beginning of smile tipped the corners of his mouth. "Indeed."

She had to admit, she quite liked the thought of being his distraction for the evening. As they spun through the dance floor, she caught a glimpse of Lucinda. Her stepsister peered at her with a long curious look before recognition came into her eyes. Ella pressed her head against Nicholas's chest, then tipped it upward to meet his astonished face.

"I, too, am trying to avoid someone," she whispered.

Mirth danced in his eyes. "Do tell, my dear."

She took the lead and danced them toward the edge of the ballroom as far from Lucinda as possible.

"The woman in the bright yellow gown," she said.

"Ah, yes. The one who looks like a giant yellow bird?" he said.

The laugh burst through her without a thought.

"I see I am correct," he replied, gripping her waist even tighter.

"She's my stepsister."

"I see. And you wish to escape her nasty glare?"

Ella chewed on her lower lip, unsure how to explain. She dropped her voice to a whisper. "I'm not supposed to be here. I wasn't allowed to come."

"Not allowed?" Shock registered on his handsome face. "I believe it was by royal decree that all eligible maidens in the land were invited and expected to attend." He paused then, tipping his head to the side, a curious and mischievous glint coming into his eyes. "You *are* an eligible maiden, aren't you?"

"Funny," she replied. "Of course, I am. It's just that I—" She snapped her mouth closed. She'd already said too much.

"Fear not, lady. Your secret is safe with me. Is Ella your real name or is it your secret identity?"

She knew he teased her and it made her giggle. "Ella is my real name," she said. "I wouldn't mind a secret identity."

"Then perhaps we'll come up with one for you."

The music ended once again, leaving them standing at the edge of the ballroom amidst other dancers. Lady Eloise pushed her way through the crowd toward them on one side. On the other, Lucinda followed by Daniella and their mother. Ella sucked in a sharp breath. Nicholas gripped her hand tight. He pulled her so close, their noses touched.

"Come with me," he whispered against her mouth.

Taking her by the hand, they fled the ballroom, leaving them all behind.

CHAPTER 6

T hey dashed toward one of the exits in the ballroom that led to the balcony. He didn't stop as he headed down the length of the balcony to a set of stairs that took them into the palace gardens. She followed him, breathless, as they descended the stairs. Her shoe slipped off her right foot.

"Oh, wait, please." She halted in the middle of the steps and turned back to grab it.

Nicholas was faster. He stepped around her and picked up the shoe from the stone step. He held it in his hands, gazing at it in wonder.

"It's made of glass," he said.

"Yes." The breathy whisper plumed white in the air.

"May I?" He held up the shoe.

Her heart pounded hard. She nodded, taking a step back to lean against the balustrade. She pulled back the voluminous skirts to expose her stocking foot. He knelt, slipping the shoe back on. A perfect fit. When he rose, he held his hand out to her again.

"I'll go slower this time," he said.

She took his hand, shivering as they descended to the ground.

"You're cold," he said.

"I'm fine."

She refused to give up this moment due to a little chill in the air. Snowflakes danced in the inky black sky as they fell in a dreamy circle to the ground. It wasn't snowing hard yet, but Ella knew the winter storms would come.

"Here." He pulled off his white gloves and handed them to her. "I don't have my cloak or I'd give that to you, too."

Uncertainty pounded through her.

"I insist," he said.

She took the gloves and slipped them on her hands. They were still warm from his body heat. It sent a thrill through her right to the tips of her toes.

They walked at a much slower pace through the moonlit rose gardens. Even during winter, the roses were fragrant and blooming. Deep blue roses lined the pathway as they wound their way through the hedges and bushes. Ahead, a greenhouse was at the end of the path.

"We can take shelter in there." He pointed to it.

She nodded, following him. She wondered who he truly was. She had never seen him before, but that didn't mean much. Ella was only allowed to visit the market or remain at the house to cook and clean for her stepmother and stepsisters.

"Do you live in the village?" he asked. He took her hand in his as he led her down the rest of the path.

"Yes," she said.

"With your stepsister?"

"Stepsisters," she said, "and stepmother."

She cringed. She was telling him way too much. He didn't need to know any more than that or that she was a servant in her own home. She quickly decided to change the subject.

"If you're not a lord, then what are you?" she asked.

He chuckled, a deep rumble in his chest. She liked the sound of it.

"I'm just a man," he said. "My friends call me Nick." He cut her a coy glance that indicated he wanted her to call him that.

"Are we friends, then?" she said.

He paused in the threshold of the greenhouse, taking both hands in his. His eyes were brilliant and bright as he looked at her. An eager affection rippled from him. It sent her senses whirling through her.

"I'd like us to be."

"I hardly know you," she whispered. Again, her words plumed in the night air.

"Then we should get to know each other."

He pulled her to stand in front of him in the doorway of the greenhouse. His body heat radiated over her, sending a warming wave through her.

"I don't know—" she began.

He placed his cold forefinger over her lips to silence her. He emitted a vitality that drew her to him. The idea of getting to know him filled her with an unexplainable happiness. He was handsome and attentive, but was that because they were at a ball caught up in the merriment and exuberance of the night?

He glanced up, meeting her eyes with a coy smile. "Look up."

Above them, a cluster of mistletoe hung from a red ribbon. Ella was certain that wasn't there a moment ago.

"Mistletoe," she said.

"You know, I've heard mistletoe is used to ward off evil spirits," he said. "And that it's also a sign of love and friendship."

Her stomach twisted with his words. Her heart fluttered wildly as she looked up at him, a twinkle of delight in his blue eyes.

"Is that so?" she asked.

"Just so." He nodded. "And, of course, there is the *other* tradition."

Kissing. There was kissing under the mistletoe. But could she allow him to kiss her? They had only just met.

He cupped her face in his cool hands.

Yes, she believed she could allow him to kiss her. Even though they had just met.

"If you'll permit me?" His warm breath fanned over her face, delighting her.

Her breath caught in her throat but she managed a reply. "I permit you."

He tipped his head to one side, leaning in, his lips a breath away from hers.

BONG.

The first clang of the clock startled her out of her reverie. She gasped and jerked away from him.

BONG.

"What's wrong?" he asked.

"I-I have to go." She pulled off his gloves, shoving them at him in a panic. Then picked up the voluminous skirts.

Before she dashed away, he caught her arm, stopping her. "Why?"

BONG.

That was three strikes from the clock.

"I'm so sorry, Nicholas. Thank you for you a wonderful evening."

She pulled her arm out of his grasp and dashed as fast as her shoes allowed. She ran up the pathway back toward the balcony steps.

"Wait, Ella!"

Footsteps behind her indicated he hurried after her. She clutched the material of her gown tighter in her hands as she ran harder. At the bottom of the steps, she hurried up.

BONG.

Four. Four strokes. What was it Noella said? She had to remove the shoes before the last stroke of midnight. But what happened if she *didn't*? At the top of the stairs, she dashed toward the open balcony door to the ballroom.

BONG.

Five. She had to hurry.

"Please, wait!" Nicholas called.

He was close behind her. She took a deep breath and dashed into the middle of the ballroom, weaving her way through the gyrating dancers and trying her hardest not to bump into any. She made direct eye contact with Lucinda, who immediately recognized her. Her eyes flew open in surprise and then narrowed. She said something to her dancing partner and pointed.

Ella had no time to pause. She pushed through the crowd, eyeing the stairs to go back up to the landing and exit the grand ballroom.

"Stop her! The woman in red! Stop!" someone shouted.

She stole a glance over her shoulder to see Nicholas entering the ballroom and imploring the others to help him stop her. Still clutching her gown in her fists, she made it to the bottom of the stairs and started up. Her legs throbbed with the exertion.

BONG.

Six and she was at the top of the stairs. She sprinted through the open door much to the surprise of the guards. They said nothing as she ran through the hallway, heading for the palace exit. Others were behind her. She heard their foot falls as they followed.

She kept her eye on the open door, her heart beating wildly. She was going to make it.

BONG.

Seven. She was out the door.

More stairs. But she couldn't stop. She headed down them. As she made her way down, her right shoe slipped off again. She paused, turned and grabbed it, and saw a group heading for her. Gasping, she turned and ran down the rest of the stairs clutching the shoe in one hand and trying not to trip over her gown.

BONG.

Eight! She hurried across the lawn to the gates. It was almost impossible to run with one shoe, but she wasn't going to take the other one off until she was clear of the gates.

BONG.

Nine and she was at the gates, her heart a furious beat. Her legs pumped madly as she made her way out of the gates.

BONG.

Ten and she was outside where she met Noella.

She stole a glance behind her to see Nicholas pause at the bottom of the stairs to search for her. When he found her, he bolted into a run.

BONG.

Eleven. Gasping, she stuck the slipper back on her foot, then hurried up the dirt road in her ball gown. As she did so, something began to happen. A warm tingling sensation spiraled through her. The world spun around and around and around like it had when she put on the shoes.

BONG.

Twelve.

And then suddenly she was floating, floating, floating, and falling, falling, falling, into a dreamy world of green and red. She flailed her arms as she fell through darkness and shadow. The snowy ground came up quickly and then suddenly everything went black.

Nicholas ran through the gates as a flash of fairy dust exploded in gold and white sparkles, leaving behind a puffy cloud of magic. He pitched forward, his hands on his knees as his breath see-sawed in and out. He was too late. Ella had disappeared and he had a good idea who was responsible.

"Well, that was exciting," a familiar voice said in the darkness.

She appeared in a puff of magic next to him, her cheeks rosy and her blue eyes bright.

"Mother, what did you do to her?" he demanded on a pant.

"I did nothing," Noella said, looking abashed. "Except give her what she wanted. A night at the Christmas ball."

"She had on glass slippers, Mother. *The* glass slippers." He stood straight, glaring at his meddlesome mother.

"Yes, well...I had to do *something* to keep them out Malvina's hands."

Frustration edged through him as he spun on his mother. He took her by the shoulders. "I saw the puff of magic in the air. Where did she go, Mother?"

"Whatever do you mean? The spell was broken at midnight and—" She gasped, putting her hands to her mouth as disbelief registered on her face. "Oh, dearest me. I think I made an error."

He huffed, his breath silver in the air.

"I forgot to remove the teleportation spell. I had thought she would remove the shoes before the last stroke of midnight. Then everything would be as it was before and the shoes would be returned to their proper place. Now, we're in a bit of a predicament."

"What does that mean? What do you mean proper place?" he demanded.

"It means, my dear son, you have to rescue her before Malvina finds her and steals those shoes." She clucked her tongue. "And I worked so hard to get them away from her. Ah, well. Nothing to do now but get the girl and the slippers back." She raised her arms, ready to do magic.

"Wait. You mean, Ella was sent to Rovenheim?"

She nodded. "Yes, dear. Quite by mistake."

"*Mother*," he said on an exasperated breath.

She ignored his irritation. "We haven't much time. First, you need to change."

She did an exaggerated wave of her arms around him and changed his clothes from formalwear into something more befitting. He was dressed in a thick tunic, pants, boots, with a sword at his waist on one side, a dagger on the other, and a heavy hooded cloak. She tapped her finger against her chin.

"Ah, yes, and you'll need a disguise. It won't do for you to go traipsing around looking like, well, *you*."

She started to wave her arm again, but Nicholas caught her wrist. "How will Ella recognize me if you disguise me?"

Thoughtful contemplation crossed her face. "My boy is so clever. Of course, you are right. Then a concealment spell instead of a disguise spell."

She cast the spell over him in a sprinkle of gold fairy dust.

"How will I find her?" he asked.

"Use your supreme tracking skills, my darling." She started to send him through to the other realm, when he stopped her again.

"How do I bring her back?"

"Ah, yes." She tapped her chin. "Now that she's in the Christmas realm, I'm not sure removing the shoes will send her back here. But give it a try, hm?"

"That's not helpful at all. How did you get the shoes in the first place?"

"Ah, that's a long story that will have to wait. Off you go, now. Good luck."

She tossed a handful of fairy dust and snapped her fingers and then he was gone.

CHAPTER 7

Malvina awoke with a start. She sat upright in her oversized, four-poster bed and stared into the inky shadows. There was nothing but dying embers left in the fireplace, plunging the cavernous room into a deep chill. Something awoke her, but she wasn't quite sure what. Some shift in the realm. As though a bit of magic rippled through the kingdom.

She shoved off the bedcovers, her bare feet landing on the cold stone floor. A shiver went up to the nape of her neck. She pulled on her thick dressing robe and stalked across her vast bedchamber where she shoved aside the tapestry hiding the Dark Mirror. It was an oval shape, set in an opulent gold frame with ornate scrollwork taking up most of the wall.

"Dark Mirror, tell me what I seek. Do I sense magic in the land?"

A fog appeared in the glass before the face appeared. A face with nothing but round holes for eyes, a nose, and mouth.

"Aye, my lovely queen. Your magic as always."

She shook her head. "Not my magic. Other magic."

The mirror paused a long moment before saying, "Aye, there is other magic, my dark queen. Seek what you have lost. The glass slippers have returned."

She sucked in a sharp breath. "The slippers have returned. I must find them. Where are they?"

"Search for them in the village. There you will find them with a young woman."

"The *village*." She said the word as if it were vile.

She hated the village this time of year. Full of cheerful, well-wishers who sang carols and wanted nothing more than peace, love, and joy. The thought made her skin crawl.

"It is where you will find the girl and the slippers."

"Then that is where I must go."

"Is she dead?" a man asked.

"She doesn't look dead," replied a woman.

"She looks dead to me," said the man.

"Poke her with a stick. See if she wakes," suggested the woman.

Ella remained still, listening to the couple. She heard a rustling nearby and then something sharp and cold hit her upper arm. She jerked upward.

"Hey!"

As she said it, the two jumped backward, recoiling from her. The woman dropped the stick.

The man was short, wearing a thick overcoat and a knit cap. He had kind eyes in his aged face. His hands were weather-worn and looked as though they had done a lot of work. The woman was a bit taller than him, with a mess of salt-and-pepper hair, a round face and a bulbous nose. Her cheeks were pink from the cold and concern was written on her face. She also wore a thick overcoat. They looked to be about the same age.

"Well, at least now we know she's not dead," said the man.

Ella glanced around. She was in a strange forest with trees rising up high into the sky. Snow drifted down in huge, heavy flakes. She no longer wore the red ballgown. She had transformed back into her tattered servant's dress. However, she still wore both of the glass slippers.

Her teeth chattered as she looked at the couple eyeing her with curiosity. The woman glanced at her feet clad in the slippers with question in her eyes.

"Wh-what happened?" Ella asked.

"We heard a boom and a crash," the man said. "Our house is just there."

He pointed over his shoulder, but Ella couldn't see the house. She pushed to a sitting position and surveyed the area. Snow fell in earnest now, coming down in thick blankets. She was baffled by the fact she still wore the glass slippers. The last thing she remembered was the clock striking midnight.

"We should get you inside, miss, before you catch your death," the woman said. "Lukas, help her up."

Lukas reached a hand down to her. She didn't hesitate as she took it. Mostly because she didn't want to freeze to death alone in the forest. She followed the couple out of the foliage.

As soon as she exited the trees, she saw the small stone cottage on the top of a hill. Gray smoke curled upward from the chimney. Each window had an inviting glow. Ivy climbed the outside of the cottage to the eaves of the thatched roof.

There were chickens in the yard pecking at the cold ground even in the snow. The woman shooed them toward the coop. A fuzzy gray cat lounged on the doorstep, its tail swishing in a lazy, contented circle.

"That's Nicodemus," Lukas said, introducing her to the cat.

He pushed open the back door and stepped over the cat. But the cat had other ideas. As soon as Lukas lifted his foot to step over him, Nicodemus sprinted through the open door. Lukas stumbled to keep from stepping on him and fell forward into the house. Ella hurried to catch him to keep him from hitting the floor. She grabbed his arm with both hands and pulled him upright. He gave her a relieved smile of thanks.

They had entered the house through the back door in the kitchen, which was small but functional. A fireplace in the living area hosted a warm fire. Nicodemus curled up on the rug in front of it, tucking his head in his front paws. An oversized chair was on one side with a well-worn cushion. A rocking chair was on the other. Next to it was a basket with several balls of yarn in it and knitting needles.

The woman followed them in, closing the door with a snap. She looked Ella up and down. "Let's get you into something, ah, warmer. What's your name, dear?"

"Ella," she said.

"I'm Agnes." She waved her to follow. "Come with me."

Agnes led her into a small bedroom with a bed covered with a thick, inviting quilt in a red and white checked pattern. A wardrobe was on one side. On the other, a stand with a pitcher and basin.

A trunk was at the end of the bed. Agnes went to it, shoving it open. After rummaging through it for a moment, she pulled out several pieces of clothing. She gave a glance to Ella with a *hmm* then nodded to herself. She placed the small stack on the bed and then turned to the wardrobe, pulling open the door. Kneeling down, she picked up a pair of boots. She pushed them into Ella's hands.

"Oh," Ella said on a breath of surprise.

"Not sure those will fit, dear, but give them a try. You can't be walking around in those." She nodded to the glass slippers. "There's a nice thick tunic and wool gown for you, too. When you get changed, come have some stew."

"Agnes, thank you."

She bustled around to the side of the bed where she struck a match and lit the lantern. It gave off a warm, inviting glow to the room.

"You're welcome, of course. And you're welcome to stay the night. It will be full on dark soon and you'll not want to be out in the cold. Do you have folks here?"

"I, uh…" Ella wasn't even sure where *here* was, but she was certain she wasn't in her home village anymore. "I'm afraid I don't."

"Ah, well, that's no never mind, then." She gave a warm smile as she exited the room and closed the door behind her.

Ella stood a moment in the room, alone, holding the boots. She shivered, a chill running through her as she realized how cold it was. She stared down at the glass slippers, wondering if they had something to do with getting her here. But if they did, how? If she took them off, would she return home? She wasn't certain, but it was worth a try.

She perched on the edge of the bed, ready to take off the slippers, but something stopped her. She hesitated, though she didn't understand why. Perhaps she shouldn't take them off? What if she did and something dreadful happened? But then, something dreadful *had* happened. She woke up in an unfamiliar forest with strangers.

Slowly, she slipped her foot out of first one slipper, then the other. And waited.

Nothing happened.

No magical whirlwind transported her away from this place. And, anyway, Agnes was right. She couldn't walk around in those slippers if she was to figure out a way out of here.

Shoving aside the thoughts of the slippers, she picked up the stack of clothes Agnes gave her which included a pair of thick socks. She was grateful for their warmth when she pulled them on. Then she removed the tattered servant's dress and cast it aside. The tunic was buttery soft and some of the finest material she had ever seen. She pulled it on, loving the feel of it against her skin. Last was the wool overdress. She smoothed her hands down the rough material. Despite that, the material was warm and toasty. Then she pulled on the boots to see if they would fit. Sure enough, they slipped on with ease.

Ella neatly folded her old dress and placed it on top of the trunk. She placed the glass slippers on top on that and stood back, thinking. Even in the half-light of the room, they sparkled. There appeared to be a shining aura around them, something she didn't understand or could explain. She was almost certain the shoes had something to do with the strange happenings as she left the palace gates and the clock struck midnight. It had to be her fairy godmother's doing. But why?

A swift knock on her door interrupted her thoughts. Agnes poked her head in a second later.

"Ah, you look much warmer. How about that stew?"

"Yes, please."

She followed the woman from the room to the kitchen where she took a seat at the old table. Agnes was all too happy to place a bowl of thick beef stew in front of her with a side of crusty bread. Lukas was busy stoking the fire and adding more wood, humming a soft tune that seemed familiar. It took Ella a moment to realize it was one of her favorite Christmas carols. One her mother used to sing.

"Lukas, come before your stew gets cold," Agnes scolded.

He placed one more piece of wood on the fire and then joined them at the table.

"It's going to be a long cold night, my wife," Lukas said. "Don't want the fire to go out."

Ella sat there, holding her spoon, as she watched the two of them interact with an abundance of love and kindness. They had both welcomed her into their home without questions, offered her warm clothes and a place to sleep. Even something to eat. It was more than her stepmother had ever done for her. It struck her then, how she had never seen it in her own household since her father disappeared from her life.

"Ella, dear, is something wrong?" Agnes asked as she spooned a bit of the stew.

Ella shook her head. "No. Everything is just as it should be."

With a smile, she dug her spoon into the stew.

CHAPTER 8

Nicholas arrived late that night in Rovenheim. But even so, the village was still alive with the ongoing boisterous celebration of the coming Christmas season. Tonight was the bonfire night, where villagers gathered around the great bonfire in the center of town, roasting marshmallows, drinking ale, singing carols, and having a merry time. Even the falling snow could not keep the most merriest away. He hoped the concealment spell his mother cast on him would keep the villagers from seeing who he truly was. There was no time to explain why he was visiting the village.

One end of the village was the enormous Christmas tree rising up into the night sky lit up with hundreds of twinkle lights. Gold garland wrapped around it from top to bottom. The Rovenheim Christmas Star sat atop it. It was the same star that had been on the tree since the first celebration hundreds of years ago.

Legend said it was placed on top of the tree by a Christmas angel and that magic made it glow with its mysterious inner light, bringing peace and harmony to a land ravaged by war and death and destruction. From that season on, things had changed. Peace reigned. The Star brought joy and happiness to all those who lived in the village. It had been a part of their celebrations for generations. He simply couldn't remember a time the Sar didn't sit atop the giant tree.

He paused a moment, scanning the crowd for Ella, but she was nowhere to be found. He decided to walk through the crowd in the hopes he would spot her. Would she still be wearing the red ballgown? If she was, she'd stand out from everyone else.

He wove in and out of people as they ate and drank and sang. His eyes flickered over every face looking for the quiet beauty with dark hair and doleful eyes. Only when they were dancing did he see a spark of life deep within her. A spark he liked to think he put there. He saw it again when he tried to kiss her under the mistletoe in the greenhouse. The mistletoe that had mysteriously appeared when he wasn't looking.

As he made his way around the far end of the village, thunder boomed overhead. Many people stopped singing to glance upward. Another boom but this time a bright red cloud followed it. When the smoke cleared, it revealed a woman clad in all black standing there. She had bright green eyes, hair the color of coal that hung in waves down her shoulders and back. She wore a tight-fitting black gown that splayed around her. It had a plunging neckline and the shoulders hosted what appeared to be black feathers. She surveyed the crowd with narrowed eyes, her dark red lips curled in a snarl. Those nearest her scurried backward to get away from her.

Nicholas knew exactly who she was.

Malvina, the self-proclaimed Queen of Darkness and Shadow in the land to the north of Rovenheim. Her dark fortress sat atop the Grimbrande Mountains. She'd been banished long ago for using her dark magic.

"Well, well," she said, her deep voice echoing through the now silent village. "It appears I was not invited to your little party."

The mayor of the village stepped forward. "We want no trouble here."

Malvina moved toward the mayor, peering down her nose at him. "Oh, but there is trouble brewing, isn't there?"

A few of the villagers exchanged worried glances. Nicholas shifted from one foot to the other. The mayor remained silent as he peered up at the dark queen.

She lowered her voice. "Where is she?"

The mayor shook his head, extending his hands as if in surrender. "Where is who?"

A tingling sensation went through Nicholas. The dark queen took a slow stroll, looking for someone. He suspected he knew who. She paused at the first young woman she came to.

"Your shoes," she said with a menacing tone. "Show me your shoes."

"M-my shoes?" the girl stammered.

"I believe my request was clear," she snapped.

The girl cut a glance to her mother standing next to her who clutched her arm. Swallowing hard, the girl lifted the hem of her skirt and showed Malvina her boots with a dusting of snow.

Nicholas edged his way around the bonfire, eyeing the village exit to the snowy forest beyond. He had to find Ella.

"What about you?" Malvina pointed at the next young woman who shivered.

Without asking, she showed the dark queen her feet. She tested several more young women until she came to a girl with blonde braids on each side of her face ending in festive red bows. When the girl failed to produce the shoes Malvina was looking for, she emitted a deep frustrated growl.

"Where is the young woman with the slippers?"

She moved through the people, who were mostly backing away.

"There is a young woman among you who has something I want. One of you knows where she is."

Her furious strides echoed through the silence as she stalked down the length of the group. The towering flames of the bonfire danced wildly behind her, casting an ominous glow matching her simmering rage. She came back to the girl with the braids, her narrowed focus fixed on her.

"And if you won't tell me where she is willingly, I will *make* you tell me."

The dark queen launched forward and wrapped her arms around the girl with the braids. Several gasped. Others cried out in fear. She spun the girl around in front of her with one arm around her waist and the other around her shoulders to keep her in place, close to her.

"This one goes with me, until such time one of you decides to confess and bring me the one with the glass slippers. And if you *don't*...I will return for another!"

She laughed and then she was gone in a puff of red smoke.

The mother of the girl with the braids cried out as if in pain and collapsed to her knees. A man, presumably her husband, kneeled beside her and patted her back, trying to calm her with quiet soothing words. But Malvina had ruined the celebratory atmosphere by stealing the girl.

A sense of hysteria and fear trickled through those left. Others had taken their children and returned to their homes, some on the outskirts of the village.

His mother had mentioned she had stolen the shoes from Malvina. Why did the dark queen want them? They must have some powerful magic inside them if she wanted them enough to steal a girl from the village.

One more scan of the gathered people, but it told him Ella wasn't there. She was a stranger to these people, after all. If there was a stranger in their midst, they would make a show of welcoming them into the fold.

He hurried to the edge of the village with no idea of how to find Ella and the glass slippers.

Ella awoke in a dreamy haze. It had been so long since she'd slept in a proper bed with proper blankets, she had forgotten how cozy it was. She burrowed deeper under the thick quilt just for a moment longer.

She'd eaten so much stew last night, she thought her stomach would burst. But it hadn't. And this morning when she awoke, she still wasn't hungry. It made her heart smile to know there was still kindness left in the world.

Or, wherever this place was.

She was fairly certain she was no longer in her world.

With a yawn and a stretch, she sat up. The tiny room was chilly but she didn't mind. She was happy she had a place to sleep that wasn't in a snowbank. She couldn't stay there forever, though. She had to figure out how to get back home. But how would she? She needed help, but she was certain neither Agnes nor Lukas would be able to help her. Where would she go? Who would she ask?

After she retired to the room last night, when she was alone, she tried calling out—softly, of course—to Noella. But her fairy godmother refused to answer. Or she wasn't able to hear her.

She pushed aside the blankets and rose. Getting out of the warm bed was difficult, but necessary. The one window in the room was covered with a thick drapery. She shoved it aside to peer out through the cold panes of glass.

The ground was covered in a thick blanket of fresh snow, glistening in the morning winter sun. She pressed her hand against the glass and shivered. It was as cold outside as it looked. She dressed, putting on the tall warm socks, the tunic and wool overdress and finally pulling on the boots. She picked up the glass slippers and her old gown and cradled them against her chest as she exited the room.

Agnes was in the kitchen humming a nameless tune. Lukas was nowhere to be found. A fire flickered in the hearth, warming the small confines of the common areas. Agnes turned from kneading her dough and smiled when she saw her.

"Good morrow, Miss Ella. How did you sleep?"

"Very well, thank you." She hesitated, glancing down at the tattered dress in her hands.

She eyed it with curiosity. "You mean to leave, don't you?"

"I can't stay here. But your kindness and generosity has meant the world to me. I also wanted to ask if you wanted these clothes back."

"Goodness, no. They belonged to my daughter. She's long gone."

"Oh," Ella gasped. "I'm sorry to hear."

She chuckled. "Oh, I meant she hasn't lived with us for years. Married herself an apothecary in the village. Has three children of her own now. Two girls and a boy." She gave a wistful sigh. "Ingrid is the oldest. She's thirteen and quite the inquisitive one. Always wears her hair in two long braids." Agnes paused to chuckle and shake her head as she thought of her granddaughter. "Listen to me going on." She waved her hand as if to wave away the thoughts. "You keep those clothes. And take this."

She wiped her hands on a kitchen towel before bustling to a tiny closet. She pulled out a long, fur lined cloak. Ella shook her head before Agnes could give it to her.

"Oh, I can't. I shouldn't," she protested.

"Why not?"

"You've given me so much already."

"Nonsense. You take this, too. You'll need it out there." She nodded toward the door.

Reluctantly, Ella took the cloak. She juggled the dress and slippers in her arms before she managed to drape it over her arm. Agnes noticed she carried her old things. A twinkle came into her eyes as if she had an idea.

"And you'll need this." She returned to the kitchen and rummaged through the pantry. She came back with a drawstring bag.

"What's that for?"

"Your clothes there." She nodded to the dress and slippers. "An old flour sack. I find them to be the most useful." She opened the top of the sack for her.

Ella placed the dress in first, then the slippers. Agnes drew up the string tight and tied a bow. It left enough slack for Ella to put the sack over her shoulder. Then she pulled on the cloak. She gave Agnes a smile.

"Thank you," Ella whispered.

Agnes kissed her cheek and gave her a quick hug. "You be careful out there. If you need us, we'll be here."

Ella nodded as the woman pulled open the cabin door. Taking a deep breath, she stepped out into the brittle morning.

CHAPTER 9

Ella began her trek from the tiny cabin through the snow that already had footprints, making it look as though there was a path. With the forest on her left, she followed the path. Every now and then she'd pass another cabin.

It felt like hours as she walked in the cold, her hands tucked into the pockets of her dress under the cloak and the flour sack banging against her hip with every step. As she neared what she suspected was the main village, the houses increased in number. The forest was still to her left but now there were houses in front of the trees.

No one was about along the row of houses. It seemed as though most everyone was in the village. Ahead, she saw a giant decorated tree twinkling with lights. Atop it was the largest, most beautiful glowing star she had ever seen. Even in the daylight, it twinkled and sparkled with its inner radiance. Her heart skipped into a happy beat and she had an overwhelming feeling of joy. A sign in faded red letters welcomed her to Rovenheim.

She paused to examine it, then glanced at the village beyond. It was a bustle of activity this morning with people hurrying along the thoroughfare. People entered and exited the shops at a frenzied pace. It was not unlike the one she frequented to purchase goods for the household. Perhaps someone in the village would be able to tell her where in the world Rovenheim was and how to return to her own small village.

She entered the fray with the throngs of people, her head swiveling from one shop to another. There was so much to see and hear. She paused to admire the huge Christmas tree rising into the morning sky wrapped in gold garland and topped with that lovely, twinkling star. It reminded her of her smaller version on the tree in her room back home.

People called to each other with waves of hello. And though the village square had festive decorations, there seemed to be a somber mood hanging over the people. Something she couldn't quite put her finger on. She listened for snippets of conversation.

"...poor woman is beside herself," someone said.

"Her eldest daughter, too," another said.

As Ella made her way through the square, she saw the sign for the apothecary. Agnes mentioned her daughter had married the apothecary. But when she made it to the shop, the sign on the door read CLOSED.

"Hear ye, hear ye!" a deep voice announced.

All those in the square stopped their activity. Ella turned to see a man standing in front of the huge Christmas tree. He was dressed in an emerald green jacket with gold buttons, black boots and a thick cloak.

"As mayor of Rovenheim," the man said, raising his voice so all heard him, "I have come to the difficult decision to cancel tonight's festivities in light of recent events."

A few gasps rippled through the crowd. Nearby, someone sniffled.

"I have also decided there will be a strict curfew for all residents at dusk for the remainder of the season," he said. "Please make sure you get your shopping done and are home before then."

Ella's brows drew together as she wondered what events occurred to cause the mayor to cancel the celebration and enact a curfew. As she pondered that, a woman brushed by her in a rush.

"Pardon me, my lady," she said on a breath and continued on in her haste.

"It's all right, but, please, before you go." Ella hurried after her, doing her best to keep up. "What event was the mayor referring to?"

The woman cut her a shocked glance. "Why, what happened last night, o'course."

"What happened? I only just arrived," Ella explained.

She stopped and turned to her, grasping her shoulder and leaning in. "A young girl was taken from the village by the queen."

Ella blinked surprise. "The queen?"

"The apothecary's daughter," she said, her voice near a whisper. "Something about slippers." She glanced around as if worried someone overheard.

The apothecary's daughter. Her heart clawed its way to her throat at the mention of that and the slippers.

"What about the slippers?" Ella asked.

The woman shrugged. "I don't know. I have to go." And she dashed off without waiting for a response.

Ella turned back to the shop and looked up at the closed sign. The queen had taken Agnes's granddaughter. All because of her slippers? That didn't make sense. Why would the queen be looking for the slippers?

Unless...

Unless the slippers were magical. She swallowed hard as she thought of the way she was whisked to the ball when she put them on. And again, when the clock struck midnight. Noella told her to remove the slippers before the last stroke of midnight. She hadn't. They had somehow transported her to Rovenheim. If she were transported here by the slippers, then that meant no one would be able to help her.

She turned from the store, pausing to watch the village square as people went about their business. No one seemed interested in her. She stood there, lost and alone trying to figure out what to do next. A foolish idea came to her. What if she took the slippers to the queen in exchange for the girl?

She didn't know where to find the queen, though.

How would she find out? How would she find this queen who had taken the apothecary's daughter? And, more importantly, *who* was the queen?

A quick glance around the bustling market told her she was not going to find answers here. No one paid her any mind as they went about their business. She worried her lower lip, fighting off the tears that sprang to her eyes.

When she was home with her stepmother and stepsisters, loneliness pressed through her then. At least there, she had someone who acknowledged her presence. Here, she was completely ignored and it cut her deep, isolating her.

Blinking furiously, she turned away from the shop and hurried back down the street. She hadn't any idea where to go other than perhaps back to Agnes, but then would she be able to help her? She had her own situation to worry about with her granddaughter captured by this queen who seemed to want Ella's slippers.

She never saw the man heading toward her until she bumped into his shoulder. She gasped, his dark coat nothing but a blur as he captured her by the upper arm.

"I'm so sorry," she whispered and tried to wrench free but he held fast.

"Ella?"

The familiar friendly voice made her snap her head up. She looked into Nicholas's handsome face. No longer was he dressed in his formalwear. Now he wore a dark brown tunic over padded pants tucked into black boots, gloves, and a thick wool cloak. A sword was strapped to his side and she thought she saw a dagger on his hip. He was well armed and looking even more handsome in his rugged clothes. Though, she admitted, he was handsome in his formalwear, too.

Relief punched through her as she sagged against him and then, without thinking, she threw her arms around his waist and hugged him.

"Nicholas! I'm so glad to see you." When she pulled back, she quickly swiped the tears from her eyes. "What are you...how are you here?"

"I've been looking for you. Are you all right?" He looked her up and down as if to inspect her.

"Yes, I'm fine. But I don't understand any of this."

He took her by the hand, leading her back to the village square. "It's a lot to take in, I'm sure. I'm glad I found you before anyone else."

"You mean the queen?"

He halted so quickly she came to a jarring halt. "What do you know about her?"

"I know she kidnapped a girl from the village. Is she looking for the glass slippers?"

"Shhh." He glanced around, concern creasing his face that someone may have overheard. "I'll explain as much as I can, but not here."

Taking her hand again, he hurried through the streets to the local tavern. The creaking sign over the door read *The Merry Elf Tavern* and something about that made her stifle a grin.

It was warm inside the tavern. On one side, a roaring fire in the hearth to keep it that way. The bar was on the other with a few patrons perched on stools nursing their ale or mead. Tables scattered around the rest of the place, which was busy with more customers who were enjoying a meal of bread and stew.

Nicholas led her to one of the tables at the back of the tavern in the corner, pulling off his cloak and draping it over the back of the chair. Ella did the same, sliding the sack off her shoulder in one fluid motion so no one would see it. Not even Nicholas. She placed it under the table at her feet just as one of the tavern maids bustled up. She placed a bowl of bread on the table in front of them.

"What'll it be?" she asked.

"Beef stew and ales for both of us," Nicholas said.

She gave a nod and hurried away. He reached for the bread in front of them and tore off a hunk while Ella waited for him to explain.

When no information was forthcoming, she finally said, "Well?"

He chewed, a thoughtful expression on his face. "I'm trying to decide where to begin."

Ella reached for the bread and tore off a piece. The soft white interior steamed with its freshness.

"Perhaps with how you got here," she suggested.

Leaning forward, he said in a soft voice, "By magic."

She lifted a brow. "Magic?"

"You doubt me?" He leaned back in the chair and popped a small piece of bread in his mouth.

The tavern maid returned with their ales and plopped the wooden steins down with a slosh. Then she dropped a slab of butter next to the somewhat demolished bread. Ella contemplated his words as she reached for the butter knife and swiped it through it, then slathered it on her bread. It had been so long since she'd had butter to go with her bread, her mouth salivated at the thought.

It made sense he was here by the use of magic. Surely, that was how she arrived because she was certain the glass slippers at her feet were magical and brought her here.

"I do not," she said at last.

He reached for the butter knife then and added butter to his next bite. "Do you...still have them?"

"The slippers?" she whispered.

He nodded.

"Yes, of course."

"But you're not wearing them," he pointed out.

"No," she agreed. "They're safe."

"Where are they?"

"At my feet," she said.

He stared at her with uncertainty, his brows drawing together in question. She smiled. "In a flour sack."

He looked her over again, as though seeing her for the first time. "Where did you get those clothes?"

Another bite as she chewed, savoring the sweet buttery taste. "When I arrived, it was nearly dark. A kind couple took me in, gave me food, and a place to sleep for the night. The next morning, the woman..." She paused, thinking of Agnes and her granddaughter. "Agnes was her name. She gave me the clothes, the boots, the cloak, and a flour sack to carry...well, you know."

He seemed twitchy about her saying the words *glass slippers* aloud, so she refrained.

"Agnes...her granddaughter was the one who was taken last night," Ella said.

"How do you know that?" he asked.

"Agnes said her daughter married the apothecary. His shop was closed today. A woman on the street told me what happened. That the apothecary's daughter was taken. I managed to put the pieces together," she said.

Before he replied, the beef stew arrived. The woman didn't linger at their table as she had other meals to deliver. Nicholas picked up the wooden spoon and stuck it in the thick stew.

"It's true," he said. "I saw it happen."

Ella stared at him from across the table, surprise flickering through her. "You were here last night?"

"Yes. Looking for you." He tore off another piece of bread and dunked it in the stew. "I'm glad I found you."

"Me, too," she whispered.

She picked up her spoon, unable to resist the delectable aroma of the beef stew. She didn't want to admit to him how relieved she was to see a familiar face. Everything she wanted to say to him sounded much too pathetic even for her own ears.

"Where is here, anyway?"

"Rovenheim," he said.

"It's quite a festive place," she said.

"This is the place where Christmas magic comes to life." He sounded proud when he said it and it gave her such a brilliant smile, she couldn't help but return it. "Ella, I'm afraid the queen will not stop until she has what she wants."

She swallowed the bite of stew and reached for her ale. "You mean, the slip—"

"Yes," he said cutting her off. "No one can know you have them."

"Why?"

"Because everyone knows she's looking for you."

"Who is *she*? This queen."

"Malvina. The Queen of Darkness and Shadow. Self-proclaimed, of course. Not a true queen. Not the ruler of Rovenheim."

"Who is then?" she asked.

"Why, the royal family, of course." When he smiled, something inside her lit up.

She liked him. A lot more than she should. She hardly knew him. But he was nice to her and seemed to really want to help her. He'd come looking for her and found her, though, one question still remained. How did he know she was in Rovenheim? She was about to ask him when the tavern door burst open. A man stood in its doorway looking frazzled.

"She's back!" he announced, and not like he was happy.

"Who does he mean?" Ella asked.

Nicholas swallowed hard and his face turned grim. "The queen."

CHAPTER 10

Nicholas threw coins on the table to pay for their meal. Then shoved his chair back. He flung his cloak around his shoulders.

"Come on."

She got up, slipping the strap of the sack over her shoulder, then pulling on her cloak to conceal it.

"Where are we going?"

"We have to get out of here," he said.

By then, the patrons of the tavern had spilled out into the street. Several were armed with swords. Outside, women gripped their daughters and hurried to get out of the village square, but it was too late. The queen stood near the enormous tree, her black dress fluttering behind her in the slight breeze. Ella lifted her hood, her heart in her throat. Nicholas pushed her behind him and armed himself with a small dagger.

"Stay behind me," he said over his shoulder.

She wasn't sure what good the dagger would do against the Queen of Darkness and Shadow, but she trusted him. More than she trusted anyone with her life.

"If I say run, then do it. Head south toward the alleyway behind the tavern."

"What about you?" She moved closer to him. So close, she smelled a woodsy scent.

"I'll find you."

Before them, Malvina lifted her arms. In a poof of red smoke, several armed guards appeared by her side blocking the entrance gate to the village. Then, with another flick of her wrist, a girl appeared in front of her. She had two long braids on each side of her head and a gag around her mouth. Her eyes were glassy with fear. Her hands were tied in front of her. Malvina placed a hand on the girl's shoulder as if to show dominance over her and as a warning to those who would try to retrieve her. One man charged. Malvina made a motion with her hand. He flew backward into the crowd, landing on the ground with a thud. The sword in his hand clattered on the cobblestones.

"If anyone else tries, you will die," she said in her dark, mellifluous voice. "Now that I have your attention." She emitted a deep laugh as she moved to stand behind the girl, placing both hands on her shoulders. "You are all under my command. You will leave when I allow it. Where are the slippers?"

Indeed, Ella sensed some powerful force over them, keeping them all rooted in place. She tried to take a step backward but it was no use.

The queen briefly surveyed the crowd, the intensity of her stare alighting on each and every face. Ella peered around Nicholas, her heart in her throat. When the queen looked right at her, she sucked in a sharp breath. Nicholas wrapped his arm around her giving her a nudge behind him once again.

"I sense the magic," the queen said. "Bring them to me and I will release the girl. If you refuse…" Her hands tightened on the girl's shoulders. She flinched, squeezing her eyes closed.

Malvina snapped her fingers. One of her guards stepped forward. She shoved the girl into his arms, then began to walk toward the crowd. Her dark, glittering eyes full of menace and disgust paused on everyone in her path.

"They are here," she said. "Somewhere among you. A young woman, perhaps. Or a young girl. It matters not to me. Give me slippers and I will return to my mountain."

Nicholas sheathed the dagger with a smooth motion that was hardly noticeable. He rested his hand on the hilt of his sword. Ella stiffened behind him. She watched his hand grip it, as though he were ready to pull it from its sheath.

Malvina made her way through the crowd paralyzed by their fear. She paused every so often to glare down at one of the younger girls. Her mother wrapped her arms around her shoulders and gripped her tight.

"You think to keep me away by adding a curfew," Malvina continued. "You think that will stop me from getting what I want?"

She shook her head, moving down the line and pausing in front of Nicholas.

Ella ducked behind him, pressing her cheek against the rough material of his cloak. A shiver of fear went through her.

"*You* have them," the queen said.

"I do not," Nicholas responded. "Why would I have a pair of slippers?"

There was a long pause. Ella peeked around his elbow. The queen's eyes narrowed to dark slits.

"Indeed, why? I sense them, though."

Nicholas's hand tightened around the hilt of his sword, his knuckles turning white.

"Here with you. You're helping her hide them, aren't you?"

Nicholas unsheathed his sword in a blur of motion. Malvina stepped back to avoid being stuck in the gut, her hands up. Surprise flickered over her face but was quickly replaced with malice. She flung her hands out toward him, punching him with a black cloud of magic.

Ella saw it happening but was too slow to move. Nicholas was lifted over her and thrown backward into the crowd. She watched in horror as he landed on the cobblestones with a grunt. Somehow, he managed to keep a grip on his sword.

Malvina reached for her then, clutching a handful of her cloak and yanking her toward her. Their noses touched and for a long, horrible moment, Ella stared into the dark, terrifying eyes of the Queen of Darkness and Shadow.

"*You.*" Her breath flickered over Ella's face. "You have them, don't you?"

"I-I—"

"Release her, you witch." Nicholas stood right behind her.

Ella's heart leapt into her throat. Malvina's head snapped up.

"I am no witch!"

"She doesn't have the slippers," Nicholas said, ignoring her. "Release her. She's not the one."

"You lie! I sense the magic of the slippers."

She jerked Ella closer, if that were even possible. Ella sucked in a breath, the death scent on the queen invading her mouth and nose. She forced away the gag that wanted to erupt. Malvina stepped backward, dragging Ella with her. With every forced step, the sack bumped against her hip with the tell-tale weight of the slippers.

"Since she won't give them up, she comes with me."

Malvina lifted her arm in a motion to release more magic. But then she jerked forward with a strangled gasp. In that one moment, her hand loosened on Ella's cloak and she stumbled away from her. Surprise flickered through her when she saw the dagger sticking out of Malvina's shoulder.

"Run!" Nicholas shouted.

Chaos erupted. When Nicholas's dagger hit Malvina, it released her dark spell holding the townsfolk hostage. Men surged forward, some wielding their swords. The women and children took off toward the south entrance of the village, putting as much distance between them and Malvina as possible.

Nicholas spun to face her where she was still frozen by fear. "Get to the alley. Now!"

Malvina's dark magic smacked into him. His face contorted in pain as he fought to stay upright. Ella didn't waste another moment. She turned and ran with the others toward the alleyway next to the tavern. Somehow, though, she felt like a coward running away from the fight even though that was exactly what he told her to do.

When she made it to the alleyway unscathed, she pressed her back against the stone wall and then peered around the corner. Men fought Malvina's guards but one still had hold of Agnes's granddaughter as he dragged her away from the fray.

Meanwhile, Malvina yanked the dagger from her shoulder and threw it to the ground. She flung more magic at Nicholas, but this time he lifted his sword. The shiny surface of the blade reflected it back to her, hitting her square in the gut.

She emitted a frustrated shout as she stumbled away. She vaulted herself into the sky, her wrath evident on her face. She glowered at the group of townspeople and then turned toward the star on the top of the tree, pausing to peer at with a mischievous grin.

"I've had enough of your cheerful, yuletide spirit," she spat, her voice dark and menacing. "And so, I will take away the symbol of your hope and joy."

In a fit of fury, she spun to the giant Christmas tree behind her and flung her magic toward the top of it.

Someone gasped. Nearby someone else shouted, "No!"

Her magic hit the twinkling star on top. There was a pop as it shattered into a thousand pieces, the light inside sparking, exploding, and then winking out as shards of glass rained down around the tree.

Malvina cackled with her glee.

"Let that serve as a warning," she said, her voice booming across the village. "Bring me the slippers or I will destroy your village and the Spirit of Christmas with it!"

And then she was gone in a cloud of red smoke. Her henchmen and Agnes's granddaughter were also gone.

Nicholas stood a long moment gazing at the tree, his gaze fixed on the top where the star previously sat and his face drained of color. The man Ella recognized as the mayor rushed over to the base of the tree, picking up the biggest shards of what was left. He held them in his hand, looking down at them with a frown.

"The Christmas Star…" The mayor's voice was soft as he ran a finger over the broken pieces. "It was the light of our season. The essence that makes Rovenheim what it is."

Nicholas sheathed his sword and stared in disbelief at the top of the tree, now devoid of the shining beacon.

Ella watched it all happen from the safety of the alley. A lump formed in her throat. The queen had destroyed the star in vengeance, because she didn't get what she wanted.

The mayor looked up at Nicholas, his face drained of color. "What are we to do now?"

Nicholas turned to him, grasped him by the arm as he looked down at the shards in his hands. "I swear to you I will find a way to mend it."

"But how?" the mayor asked, his face drawn with grief.

He shook his head. "I don't know yet. Save the pieces for me."

The mayor nodded as he turned to pick up the remaining pieces, even though some were no more than tiny shards.

"Nicholas?"

Leaving behind the comforting shadows of the alley, Ella's heart raced with a mix of surprise and uncertainty. Her eyes narrowed in confusion, searching for answers as she studied his face. The lines on her forehead deepened into a puzzled frown, reflecting her bewilderment at witnessing the encounter between him and the mayor.

He hurried over to her, pulling her into a fierce hug.

"Are you all right?" he breathed into her hair.

"Yes, I'm fine."

But she had never felt so helpless as she did watching the horror of Malvina's attack unfold.

"We need to get out of the village." He took her by the hand and led her back into the alley. "It's not safe for you here."

"Where are we going? The alley is a dead end," she said.

"Is it?"

He quirked a grin as he paused at the wall at the back of the alley. He pressed a stone near the middle. It sank into the wall and, a moment later, a small door slid open.

"Watch your head." He released her and ducked under the doorway, disappearing on the other side.

Taking a deep breath, Ella followed. On the other side, he depressed another stone, closing the door. They stood on the edge of a forest surrounded by foliage. The stone wall of the alleyway was at their backs. Snow drifted down, coating the trees in a light dusting.

"Stay close," he said and started down the length of the wall to the south.

"Where are you taking me?"

"Into the wild. Where it's safe."

"It's safe in the wild? But it's snowing. And it's cold. What about shelter? And food?"

"Don't worry," he said, sounding reassuring. "I'll take care of you."

"But—"

He turned to her, placed a gloved finger over her lips. He gave her a small smile. "Trust me. Can you?"

She didn't know why, but she did. She nodded slowly. "Yes."

"Good. We'll be in shelter before night falls."

He started walking again down the length of the wall. She kept close, stepping where he stepped and making sure she didn't lose sight of him in front of her. The sun was already dipping toward the horizon, bringing on colder temperatures and a frigid night. She hoped he was right in that they would have shelter by night, because she certainly didn't want to freeze to death in this strange land.

CHAPTER 11

Ella shivered under the thick cloak, despite its warmth. She pulled the hood down on her head and bowed it to keep the falling snow out of her face. They'd been walking for hours. At some point, the wall of the city had ended, leaving them in the thick forest with nothing but trees and bracken and more trees. As the day turned into night, snow fell thicker and heavier. Her breath plumed white in front of her.

Nicholas glanced back to make sure she was keeping up. "We're almost there."

"Almost where?"

"There's an abandoned cabin ahead." He waved ahead of him.

"How do you know?" She was leery of his information as she squinted into the distance, as if that would help her see better. She saw nothing but trees and shadows and snow.

He grinned. "I know these woods."

If he was walking a path, she was unable to see it. But she followed him, the bag bouncing against her hip every so often when she took a misstep. At last, the trees seemed to thin and there was a small clearing. In the distance, a cabin. All the windows were dark, so it was safe to assume this was the abandoned cabin he mentioned. She was relieved to see it, to know they were coming to the end of their hike and they'd be in shelter for the night.

But then, what would tomorrow bring?

"Where are we going?" she asked.

"To the cabin," he said.

"No, I mean, *after* that. What is our destination?"

He paused, turning toward her in the shadowy moonlight. "I'm taking you to safety while I work on a way to get you home."

Her brows drew together. "Where is safety?"

"The royal castle."

She stared at him in shocked silence. He turned back and continued on but she had more unanswered questions.

Nicholas's boots left deep tracks in the snow. She did her best to step in them and follow, quite literally, in his footsteps. He hurried up the creaky wood steps of the porch. He swung the door open and stepped aside, waiting for her to enter.

Once she was inside and he closed the door behind her, they were plunged into darkness. Ella clutched her elbows and tried not to shiver. Even though they were out of the elements, it was freezing inside the cabin.

"I'll get a fire started."

He struck a match and lit an oil lamp near the door. It bathed the small one-room cabin in a pale-yellow light. On one side was the fireplace. On the other an old, tattered sofa that had seen better days. Behind it, a narrow bed with a stack of blankets neatly folded on the end of it. In front of them, a small kitchen that didn't offer much. Only a sink. No stove.

Next to the fireplace was a full log rack. As if someone had chopped wood one day and then disappeared the next. Nicholas set about placing the logs in the fireplace. He struck another match and held it to the end of one log. A tiny flame started. He did the same on the other end.

She wandered into the kitchen. The overhead cupboards had seen better days. They were covered in dust and cobwebs. She pulled one open. Empty. She was glad they had the hearty beef stew and bread earlier that day, but she was still a little hungry.

"There. That should warm us up in no time. Are you hungry?" he asked, as if reading her thoughts.

"Not really," she lied. Since there were no provisions here, she didn't want him to feel as though he had to provide for her. He already did that at the tavern, after all.

He moved to the bed and picked up the top blanket. He shook it out. Dust clouded in the air around him, making him cough and sneeze. Once he had the dust out of that one, he picked up the one under it and shook it out. It wasn't as dusty as the top one. Then he handed one of them to her.

"These blankets should keep us warm by the fire," he said.

"Thank you."

She didn't want to remove her cloak yet. But she was tired of carrying the bag with the slippers. She slid it off her shoulder and placed it on the edge of the sofa. Then she grabbed one of the better-looking cushions and tossed it to the floor by the fire. She wrapped the blanket around her shoulders and plopped down on the cushion, watching as the flames took off.

Nicholas did the same. He placed a cushion across from her and dropped the thick blanket. Then eyed the bag on the edge of the sofa.

He pointed to it. "May I?"

She nodded.

He opened it and pulled out one of the glass slippers. He held it up to the firelight, watching as the rainbow of colors danced in the glass. He reached in the bag and grabbed the other one, inspecting it much the same way.

"Remarkable," he muttered.

"Are they?" she asked.

"Well, yes. Not a scratch or crack on them." Gently, he returned them to the bag.

She chewed her lower lip. "Nicholas, I think there is much we need to discuss."

He moved to sit on the cushion. "There is?"

"Isn't there? I have many questions," she said.

Like, how did the slippers bring her here? How would she get home? Why did the queen want the slippers? And if he arrived by magic, could he then return to her world by the same magic? They had only just begun to discuss everything at the tavern when they were interrupted and Malvina arrived.

He took a deep breath, expelled it. He picked up the poker and nudged one of the logs to encourage it to continue to burn. "Yes, I know you do."

She waited with her hands clasped in her lap and watched him. A pensive expression was creased on his handsome face as he searched for the words.

"Have you tried to use the slippers to return home?" he asked suddenly.

"How would I do that?" she wanted to know.

He rose, reached for the bag and brought it to her. "Try them on. I have an idea."

Her brows drew together in suspicion, but she took the bag from him nonetheless. Placing it in front of her, she pulled off her boots and her thick socks. She slipped the shoes out of the bag. She put one on, then the other.

"Now what?" she asked.

He held a hand down to her. She grasped it as he pulled her to her feet. She pitched forward a little. He caught her in his arms. Heat fluttered to her face as he held her for that brief moment as he set her back on her feet. She straightened, smoothing her suddenly damp palms down the front of her cloak.

He took one of her hands in his. She hoped he didn't notice the dampness.

"Close your eyes," he said.

"Why?" Now she was suspicious.

"Humor me. Please."

She did as he asked. Then he said, "Now think of your home. Picture it the way you remember it. Are you seeing it in your mind?"

She nodded.

"Tap your heels together."

She cracked one eye to glare at him. He gave her an encouraging nod. She closed her eye again and tapped her heels together once.

Nothing happened.

The crackling fire was the only sound in the silence. Her eyes were still closed as he released her hand. She heard the swish of his clothes and then he gripped her by the upper arms. His touch was gentle but firm.

"Try again," he said.

"This is ridiculous," she said.

"Once more. For me?"

She sighed. She pictured the home she shared with her step-mother and stepsisters. Living in the drafty third-floor bedroom. Cooking and cleaning and doing all the things they made her do. The only happy memories she had was when her father was still alive and those were becoming more and more distant.

She clicked her heels together again.

Still nothing.

She opened her eyes and met his blue gaze. Firelight danced in the depths. Finally, he dropped his arms to his side.

"Well, it was worth a try anyway." He gave her a weak smile as he plopped down on the cushion.

She lowered herself down and pulled off the slippers, placing them on the floor in front of her. She pulled on her thick socks, but left her boots off.

"What did you think was going to happen?" she asked.

"I was hoping it would send you—us—home."

"Is that why you took me by the arms?"

"Yes. I thought it would help."

The firelight danced in his chestnut hair, making some of the strands appear gold. "Why does Malvina want the slippers?"

"Because they are powerful," Nicholas said.

Ella snorted uncertainty. "Are they?"

A ghost of a smile flickered over his face. "They are. For someone who knows how to use the magic inside them."

She eyed them, wondering what sort of magic they truly had. Why wasn't she able to use the magic inside them to go home? Because she, herself, did not have magic?

"And I don't know how to use the magic inside them," she said.

He pressed his lips together in a thin line and shook his head.

"So, how are we going to get back?" she asked.

Absently, he poked the fire. He looked thoughtful, working on how to answer her.

"You don't know, do you?" she said.

He shook his head. "Not yet. I'm working on a plan."

She thought of her fairy godmother, Noella. If she could call her, get in contact with her somehow, then perhaps she would be able to help them.

"What about Noella?"

His head snapped up. He stiffened and went still as he peered at her. "What about her?"

"She said she was my fairy godmother." She clamped her mouth shut then, pressing her lips together. She'd said too much.

He tipped his head to one side, question flickering across his face. "Your fairy godmother."

She emitted a nervous laugh. "I know it sounds silly but...she...I think she had something to do with me coming here."

And the ball, but she didn't want to talk about that. She didn't want to tell him the woman had used some sort of magic to dress her and get her there. And even though she didn't want to admit the same magic brought her to Rovenheim, there was no denying that it did and the slippers had something to do with it.

"I don't think your fairy godmother can help us," he said. "I have a feeling we're on our own."

Her previous idea of handing over the slippers to Malvina in exchange for the girl still seemed like an option. She dragged her lower lip through her teeth.

"What about the girl Malvina kidnapped?" she asked.

"What about her?"

"Well, don't you think we should do something about that?"

He blinked as he looked at her, as if he didn't believe she suggested such a thing.

"Malvina still has her," Ella went on. "Perhaps if we take the slippers in exchange for the girl—"

"No," he snapped. "Malvina cannot have the slippers."

"Why not?"

"Her magic is too powerful."

"Well, what does she plan to do with them?" Ella asked.

He remained silent. Something about the way he looked made her think he *knew* what the Queen of Darkness and Shadow intended to do with them.

"We cannot give her the slippers," he said in a cagey response.

"But what about the girl? We can't just leave her. We have to do something." What, she didn't know, but her conviction was strong that they should rescue her.

"I'll think about it," he said, poking the fire again. "We should get some sleep. In the morning, I'll find something for us to eat and some water."

Ella wrapped the blanket tighter around her frame as she moved to lay down, her head on the cushion. She wasn't certain she had convinced Nicholas. Not yet. In the morning, she would try again. And, truth be told, she was exhausted from the day. Her eyes were heavy and before she knew it, she was fast asleep.

CHAPTER 12

Nicholas poked the fire, pushing the logs together until the flames went higher and higher. When Ella's breathing went deep and he was sure she was asleep, he put aside the poker.

So, his mother had posed as her fairy godmother? No doubt to get her to the ball, but why? Why would his mother do such a thing? He needed to talk to her.

He rose to his full height, taking care not to disturb Ella as she slept. He crept to the cabin door and twisted the knob slowly, keeping a watchful eye on her sleeping form. When he was certain she hadn't been disturbed, he pulled open the door with a soft creak. He held his breath, glancing back at Ella but she hadn't moved.

Blowing out the breath, he closed the door behind him with a soft snick and stood on the porch. The woods were silent as snow fell in earnest, blanketing the ground in a thick layer. It would make tomorrow's travel more difficult.

"Mother?" he whispered into the night. His breath fogged with his words. "Where are you?"

A few moments of silence passed. He walked down the length of the porch to the railing as far from the door as possible. He tried again.

"*Mother*, where are you?"

"Right here, dear." Her voice was behind him.

He spun to face her. Her hair sparkled in the half-light of the porch. She wore a thick white cloak with a fur collar, fur at the sleeves and around the hem. Her hands were covered in white gloves. She looked as though she'd appeared out of a winter dream.

"Sh. Don't wake Ella."

She glanced around, surprise and delight plastered on her face. "Ella? You found her? Where is she?"

"Inside." He gripped her by the shoulders. "And, yes, I found her. Now tell me how to get back to her world."

"Does she have the slippers?" she asked, worry lines creasing her forehead.

"Yes, she does. Mother—"

"Thank goodness." She pressed a hand against her chest and moved away from him, forcing him to release her. "I was worried they would fall into Malvina's hands."

"They almost did. Malvina knows she has them."

"Oh, dear. That's not good at all."

"No, and Malvina has kidnapped a young girl from the village and..." He paused, raking his hand over his face as he chose his words. "She destroyed the Christmas Star."

"No!" She gasped, covering her mouth with a gloved hand.

"That's not the worst of it." His stomach churned as he stepped closer. "Mother, she said if we didn't bring her the slippers, she would destroy the village and the Spirit of Christmas."

Her face blanched for a moment before she regained her composure. She dropped her hand and turned away, facing the falling snow.

"That's ridiculous. She wouldn't hurt me."

"Are you certain?" he demanded. "She wants the slippers no matter the cost. Mother, you have to tell me how to return Ella to her world. It's the safest place for her *and* the slippers."

She turned to face him, a mischievous glint in her eyes. "I'm afraid I can't do that, my dear."

He huffed out a frustrated breath, folding his arms across his chest. "Why not?"

"Because you have to find your own way." She gave a weak little smile.

His eyes narrowed in suspicion. "Is this some sort of test?"

She blinked, giving him her best innocent look. "Whatever do you mean?"

"She told me you were her fairy godmother," he said. "Care to explain *that*?"

"Oh...well, that *might* be true." She moved to the railing, gazing out at the falling snow, but she didn't elaborate. "It's so peaceful here, isn't it?"

"Did you send her to the ball?" he asked, his tone demanding.

She cut him a sideways glance and bit her lip. Guilt washed over her face.

"You *did*!" He huffed and ran a hand through his hair. "Why?"

When she said nothing, he began to pace. "For the same reason you sent me? You planned this whole thing, didn't you?"

She spun to face him, her cloak swishing around her. "I only want the best for you."

"The best being, what...?"

"Well, it's clear there is no one here in Rovenheim for you. You needed a little push."

"A push you willingly gave me." Fury flickered through him. "You lied to me."

She shook her head. "I never lied. I told you there was a Christmas ball that needed some holiday magic. You delivered."

Again, he folded his arms across his chest. "And how did I do that?"

She waved toward the cabin where Ella slept. "You gave it to her. If it hadn't been for that pesky clock tower clanging its midnight bell, you would have kissed her and then—" She clamped her lips shut.

Suspicion lanced through him. The only way she knew he was about to kiss Ella was if she spied on them. "You were responsible for the mistletoe. And then *what*, Mother?"

She waved away the thought. "I simply must go, my darling. I'm needed at a yuletide celebration in Wickershire." She gave him a quick peck on the cheek.

"No, Mother—"

But she poofed away in a cloud of pale blue smoke. He disliked her cagey responses to all of his questions. He should have known she was up to something when she insisted he attend the Christmas ball in Whitebridge.

His mother, as he knew, was determined to spread her Christmas cheer to every kingdom and village within her power. Likely why she insisted on him going to that ball in the first place. Also, likely why she flitted off to Wickershire, wherever that was. She was the Spirit of Christmas, after all. But then, things were not going well in Rovenheim, so why wouldn't she stay and help him?

Unless she expected him to figure it all out on his own. The destruction of the Christmas Star atop the tree in the village square was more devastating than he cared to admit. Add that to the mystery of the slippers and getting Ella back to her world, he wasn't sure where to begin.

He paused at the railing, watching the snow fall in the peaceful night. Slivers of moonlight filtered through the treetops making the snow glisten under its pale light.

Taking Ella to the castle might not be the best idea, but it was the only one he had and the only place he thought she would be safest. He was aware the moment he stepped onto the castle grounds, the concealment spell his mother put on him to hide his identity would be reversed. His true identity would be visible to all those in the castle. When they arrived, how would he explain the servants calling him highness?

He shoved away the thought. He'd worry about that later and instead turned his thoughts to the young girl Malvina kidnapped. Perhaps Ella was right. They should rescue her. The thought of her being a prisoner at the hands of the dark queen didn't sit well with him. But they couldn't exchange the slippers for her. There had to be some other way to get the girl back and keep the slippers out of Malvina's hands.

But how?

The cold pressed into him and with a shiver, he stepped back to the door. He twisted the knob and opened it, peeking through to make sure she still slept. She hadn't moved at all. The fire was starting die. He closed the door behind him and stepped to the fireplace. Picking up the poker, he pushed the logs around until the flames reignited. He sat on his cushion staring into the fire, determined to find a way to rescue the girl from Malvina and get Ella home.

How, he didn't know yet.

Ella woke with a start. Disoriented, she sat up, her heart pounding a wild beat. It took several moments to realize where she was. Next to her, Nicholas still slept in front of the fire which was now nothing more than embers.

She had personal needs to tend and pushed to her feet. As she turned to the small kitchen, she gasped and gaped at it. She rubbed her eyes to make sure she wasn't seeing things.

But no.

The small kitchen that was nothing more than a few empty cabinets was now a full kitchen with a spread of food. She glanced back at Nicholas who slept on.

She crept into the area trying to understand. A silver tray was piled high with biscuits. Another with scones. There was a wheel a cheese, a loaf of bread, and even out of season fruit.

Behind her, Nicholas yawned and stretched. She spun to face him.

"Did you do this?" She waved to the food.

Confused, he got to his feet to see what she was talking about. He took two steps then halted, staring at the food. Confusion passed over his face before he controlled it.

"I'd like to say I did, but no."

"Then who?"

He cracked a smile. "Ella, surly you believe in magic by now."

He reached up and brushed her cheek. As a reflex, she jerked back. He dropped his hand back to his side.

"I'm sorry," he said. "You have something on your face."

There was no looking glass to be found. "I-I do?"

He reached into his pocket and brought out a kerchief. "On your cheeks. It looks like you were too close to the fire."

She took the kerchief and wiped at her cheeks, hoping she got it all. When he chuckled, he gently pulled the material out of her hand.

"May I?"

Her heart thudded. She nodded.

Taking the kerchief, he brushed her cheeks with gentle pressure. She kept her eyes off of his for fear of looking into them and seeing something she wasn't prepared to see. He was kind and gentle and it was something she wasn't used to. When he finished, he tucked the soiled kerchief back into his pocket.

"There. All gone. Shall we eat? We'll need food if we're to go to Malvina's lair and rescue the girl."

A broad smile crossed her lips. "We're going to rescue her?"

He nodded. "Yes. I thought about what you said and you're right. We have to do something. Do you know her name?"

"Ingrid," she said. "I think her name is Ingrid."

She thought of Agnes, then, and wondered how she was taking the news her granddaughter had been kidnapped by the dark queen. For a moment, the fear Agnes would give her up crossed her mind, knowing she had the glass slippers. But then, would she betray her in such a way? She wasn't sure, and it was a real cause for concern.

Shoving that thought aside, she decided worry about something out of her control was senseless.

"Good, then we'll see if we can get Ingrid out of Malvina's hands and returned to the village where she belongs."

Ella picked up one of the scones and broke off a corner. She popped it into her mouth, chewing thoughtfully.

"Do you know where Malvina is?" she asked.

"I do," he said. "But it will not be an easy trek. And the mountain pass is particularly treacherous this time of year. We'll need help." He picked up a biscuit and broke it in half. "And we'll need provisions." He paused, looking over the pile of pastries. "Something other than sweets."

"And," she said around a mouthful, "a plan for keeping the slippers."

"The slippers are the least of my concerns." He paced the small confines of the cabin. "Malvina destroyed the Christmas Star atop the village tree. We'll need to find a way to repair that, too."

"It's that important?" she asked.

He nodded. "It's the heart of Rovenheim. It's what makes our season merry and bright."

She tipped her head to the side as she considered his words. "I always thought how people felt about the season made it merry and bright. Not necessarily because of an object."

His brows drew together. "What do you mean?"

"I mean that the magic of the season is within. That it really isn't about parties or decorating or gift-giving. That it's about doing nice things for the people you love and spending time with those people."

She broke off another piece of the scone as she peered up at him through her lashes. She thought of past Christmases with her father. On the eve before the holiday, they would sit together by the fireplace, with all the candles lit, after a hearty meal of roasted duck and vegetables, and he would read to her *The Night Before Christmas*. She'd leave a plate of cookies out for the Christmas elf for when he delivered their packages. Afterward, her father would tuck her into bed and wish her a happy Christmas and pleasant magical dreams and then kiss her on the forehead.

That was before he married Lillian. Before she and her two, dreadful daughters moved in with them and ruined all their holiday plans. Before her father left and never returned.

"Are you all right?" he asked.

"Yes, of course. Why do you ask?"

Contemplation crossed his face. "It's just that, for a moment, you had the saddest look."

She forced a smile. "I'm fine."

"I think you're right, though. That doing things for the people you love and being kind is part of the season. But the Christmas Star was unique. It pulled us together when the outlook for the world was bleak. Centuries ago, it brought peace to our war-ravaged country."

"Oh." The word came out as a delicate whisper. "Then I understand why you want to repair it."

He ate the rest of the biscuit and then brushed crumbs from his hands. "Well, shall we go? We have another day's trek but should be at the castle by nightfall."

She finished her scone and nodded, wishing she had a pot of tea to wash it all down. She pulled on her boots and slipped the flour sack with the slippers and the tattered dress over her shoulder, then wrapped the cloak around her. One last glance back at the spread of food and her stomach rumbled again.

With a sheepish glance at Nicholas, she wrapped up several of the pastries in a piece of cloth. He chuckled as he paused at the door, waiting for her.

"They are delicious, aren't they?" he asked.

Nodding, she tucked the small package into the flour sack on top of the shoes. "They are."

He pulled open the door to the bright morning sun and the snow glistening on the ground. She followed him out into the crisp air, her stomach giving a lurch. Excitement and apprehension flickered through her at the thought of arriving at the royal castle that evening.

CHAPTER 13

It was a long trek through the trees. They finally broke free of the forest and headed up a slope of a hill, the sun glinting off the snow. Her legs burned from the exertion and her breath see-sawed in and out of her, pluming in front of her. She spotted a cluster of rocks ahead and headed for them.

"Please, I need a moment." She paused, pressing a hand against her side to catch her breath. She leaned against the rock to give her tired legs time to stop aching.

Nicholas halted and turned to face her, stepping closer with an encouraging grin. "It's not far now."

"Good." She pulled out the cloth wrapped around the pastries as her stomach grumbled. She handed him a biscuit, which he accepted with a grateful smile.

"We can get something to eat there when we arrive," he said.

She broke off a piece of scone, examining the baked blueberries inside. "Will they allow that?"

"Of course, they will," he said around a mouthful. "Why wouldn't they?"

She peered up at him under her lashes. "It seems odd they would allow that for commoners like us."

He chuckled. "They will be glad to serve us."

She tipped her head to one side. What a curious thing to say. How did he know this? He seemed sure the royal family would be happy to take care of travel weary visitors.

"Besides, the king and queen are not in residence this time of year," he added.

"Oh?" She popped the small piece of scone in her mouth and chewed.

He nodded. "They both have duties elsewhere they have to attend."

"Then who's left in charge?" she asked, genuinely curious, for she never understood how those things worked.

"There's a steward who takes care of things when the royal family is not in residence." He took another bite of the biscuit.

There was something niggling at her about the way he said it with such confidence. As if he knew and understood the inner workings of the home of the king and queen of Rovenheim.

"Do you really think Malvina will destroy the village if she doesn't get what she wants?"

He paused, his mind working as he held the half-eaten biscuit. "I hope not, though I certainly wouldn't put it past her. She dislikes this time of year."

"Why?" She simply couldn't fathom anyone disliking this magical time of year.

He gave her a faint smile and ate the rest of the biscuit. "She has darkness in her heart. Let's keep going."

She followed him as she finished her scone. Now that she rested, she felt as though she was able to continue.

As they crested the hill, she saw the gleaming towers outlined against the brilliant blue sky in the distance. She assumed this was the royal castle and their destination and her heart quickened. It was nothing like the royal palace back home.

No, this was grander with tall white towers glistening against the evening sun. The heraldry flags were stiff in the breeze at the top of three turrets in bright, cheerful colors of red and green plaid, reminding her of the bow that was wrapped around the box the glass slippers were in.

"Is that the royal castle?" she asked.

"Yes, Rovenheim Castle." He turned to her and grasped her hand. "Not long now."

Her heart thudded hard as they continued on their way. The closer they got, the quicker he picked up the pace. He seemed to be ready to be there.

As the sun dipped toward the horizon, and the sack bounced against her aching hip, she realized she, too, was ready to be there. The castle was made of white marble, shining in the waning light as though it were a welcoming beacon to all who approached.

Around the castle, a wall made of white stone and look-out turrets every several feet for guards. An iron gate was opened, welcoming travelers. Beyond the gate, she couldn't see much but she heard happy voices raised in song. She cut a glance to Nicholas, who had a faint smile on his face, his cheeks and the tip of his nose were ruddy from the cold. There was no mistaking the joy on his face as he approached the gate at a wicked pace. It was almost as though he forced himself not to break into a run.

As they approached, she looked up at nearest tower and saw two guards standing on the edge of the wall peering down. Their helms hid most of their faces. They were dressed in full armor with thick cloaks around their shoulders to ward off the cold. A sword was strapped to each of their sides and they both held bows at the ready.

One gave a nod to them as they passed. A quick glance at Nicholas as he nodded back and gave a brief wave. The guards seemed unconcerned with his arrival. Almost as though they knew him.

Perhaps they did. Perhaps Nicholas was well traveled and had been here before. There was much she didn't know about him and yet she was willing to trust him with her life.

As they entered through the gate, she took in the surroundings. There were people milling about doing chores and taking care of animals. One side boasted a twenty-foot tree decorated in gold and plaid ribbon for the holiday. A gold star sat atop it. She gasped when she saw it.

"The tree is magnificent, isn't it?" he asked. "My fa—er, the king has one brought from the countryside every season."

"It's wonderful," she breathed, her breath pluming in front of her.

He leaned toward her and dropped his voice, "Wait until you see it lit up tonight."

His warm breath brushed her cheek as he spoke, sending a wave of delicious longing through her. She gave him a quick glance as he winked and pulled her along.

"Your highness! You've returned!" a rotund, jovial man shouted with an exaggerated wave of his arm.

He had thinning black hair showing off his shiny pate and bright blue eyes that flashed with surprise and glee as he hurried across the courtyard to greet them. His fur-lined cloak flapped behind him. His black boots were coated with snow. The tips of his ears were red, as well as his nose and cheeks, from the frosty air. She pulled Nicholas to a jarring halt and jerked her hand from his as shock rolled through her.

"*Your highness?*" she repeated under her breath.

He gave her a sheepish grin. "Yes, I wanted to tell you, but—"

The man skidded to a halt in front of them, taking Nicholas into a giant bear hug and squeezing him in his beefy arms. He pulled back, a broad grin on his face as he held him at arm's length. He gave a belly laugh of surprise and delight.

"We didn't expect you back yet."

Then he noticed Ella.

"Oh, my. Who is this lovely lady? Forgive me, my lady, I didn't see you there." As he bowed, he took her hand in his gloved one.

"This is Ella," Nicholas said. "Ella, this is Magnus, he's the steward of the castle when the royal family is away."

Magnus bent and placed a gentle kiss on the back of her hand. "My dear, your hands are frozen." Then he turned a scalding gaze on Nicholas. "Your highness, have you no chivalry? Why didn't you give the girl gloves?"

"There was no time. We were in a bit of a rush when we left the village."

His expression turned to one of concern. "Oh, yes, we heard what happened in the village. That Malvina destroyed the Christmas Star. Whatever will we do now?" His face contorted into agonized lines.

Magnus was, by far, the most expressive person Ella had ever met.

"I have a plan."

Nicholas cut her a glance as she shifted from one foot to the other and withdrew her hand discreetly from Magnus's.

"But we can discuss that in good time. I'm frozen to my toes. Let's go inside." He waved them toward the entrance.

"Yes, of course. I'll have a chamber made up for the lady."

They entered the castle through the double oak doors with the wrought iron hinges and paused in the massive foyer. There was so much to see, Ella wasn't sure where to look first. From the black and white checkered floor covered in thick, plush ancient rugs to a wide curved staircase that went up to the second level to the yawning doorway to their right leading into what appeared to be the great hall. There was a long, wooden table that seated twenty on each side and one at each end. Behind that, an oversized fireplace that boasted a roaring fire, the light flickering off the floor and the stone walls giving it a warm and inviting ambience. To their left, another room that boasted plush and comfortable furniture, another fireplace, plush rugs, and oil paintings on every wall.

Everywhere she looked were holiday decorations. Green garland trimmed in red and gold ribbon wound around the banister. A giant tree adorned with red and gold tinsel, red and gold ornaments, and tiny white twinkling lights was on the far wall in the great hall. Greenery and candles decorated the fireplace mantle. She had never seen such a holiday splendor in her life and it made her smile.

Everything seemed bigger and brighter here in Rovenheim Castle.

"In the west wing, if you please, Magnus," he said, oblivious to her gawking.

"The west wing, your highness?" Magnus gaped openly from Nicholas to her and back again, as if he couldn't believe the request.

"Yes, Magnus. The *west* wing."

The man nodded. "Very well." He turned to Ella then and gave her a bright smile. "I'll have a bath brought up to you so you can thaw out."

"Oh, that sounds lovely." The thought of a steaming bath after all the travel through the cold and the snow made her warm just thinking about it.

"And some warm clothes, too," Nicholas added. "She'll need some traveling clothes."

"But this is fine." She waved to the gown Agnes gave her, feeling as though he thought her secondhand clothes weren't good enough.

"You'll need something warmer if we're to travel to the Grimbrande Mountains."

As they spoke, several servants scurried up the stairs. Magnus gave them a cursory glance and then turned his attention back to Nicholas.

"The Grimbrande?" Magnus exclaimed. "But, highness—"

Ella glanced from the steward to Nicholas. Magnus clearly had objections to the idea of them going to the Grimbrande Mountains. Objections which Nicholas didn't want to hear.

"We will discuss *later*," he said through his teeth, cutting him off. "Right now, Ella and I are famished."

Even as he said it, her stomach rumbled. The two scones she'd managed to eat were long gone.

Magnus straightened and gave him a sharp nod. "Would you like to feast in the dining hall?" He motioned to the cavernous room to the right.

"In my chamber, if you please." He held his hand out to her. "And then I'll escort Ella to hers afterward."

"Very good. I'll have the meal brought up right away."

Ella hesitated a moment as she watched Magnus hurry away.

"Come, Ella," Nicholas said, still extending his hand to her.

She folded her arms over her chest, taking a step away from him. Here she was with a *prince* all this time. He must think she was nothing but a naïve dolt as they traipsed through the forest and the snow to get to the castle. And why bring her here? He did say he thought it was the safest place for her.

But all that changed when they decided to rescue Ingrid from the dark queen.

"Not until you tell me who you really are, *your highness*."

He flushed, his cheeks turning a dark pink as he clenched his jaw. He gave her a slow nod. "You're right, of course. I should have told you from the start."

Her eyes narrowed as she peered at him. "Are you a prince, then?"

It was almost as if she didn't believe it.

"I am," he said, his voice low and quiet.

Her arms dropped to her side as she gaped at him. She spun away from him, facing the roaring fire and the decorated tree in the great hall. When she went to the ball at the palace, it had never occurred to her she would dance with a prince. In fact, she hadn't expected to see the prince at all. At least, the prince she knew from her own world. Instead, she had danced and jested with the prince of Rovenheim. And he had almost kissed her.

She shoved that thought away, trying to remain in touch with her ire. "You lied to me."

"Well, I never actually told you I was a prince," he said.

She frowned at him over her shoulder. "You lied by omission. That's the same as lying."

He spread his hands as if in surrender. "Ella, please understand—"

She turned on him. "Why were you at Whitebridge Palace?"

"I was attending the ball, the same as you." He looked flustered, as though he didn't understand why she was asking.

"Did you run into me on purpose?" she demanded, propping her hands on her hips.

"Ah, if I recall, my lady, you were the one who ran into *me*." He grinned at her.

Heat pounded through her, pushing all the way to the roots of her hair as she blushed. Yes, of course, he was right. She *had* run into him. He took a tentative step toward her, moving slowly with his hands still out.

"Ella, I didn't tell you at the ball because…well, at the time it didn't seem relevant. And then you ran away and I didn't think I would ever see you again," he said.

She dropped her arms and moved a little closer. "Did my fairy godmother send you here, too?"

His face was impassive for a long moment as he decided how to answer. "She insisted I come after you and find a way to return you back to your realm."

"Why did you bring me here when you knew I would discover your identity?" she asked.

"Initially, I wanted to bring you here because I knew you would be safe from Malvina. But then we decided to rescue Ingrid and things changed. If we're to trek up the mountains, we need provisions. This was the only place I could think to get those provisions. Plus, we can take horses and not go on foot." He took another tentative step toward her, closing the gap between them. "Can you forgive me for not telling you the whole truth?"

"Is your name really Nicholas?" she asked, her eyes narrowed to slits.

He chuckled. "Yes, it is."

She took a deep breath, expelled it. "Then I suppose I can."

He held his hand out to her once more. "Come. Let's get something to eat and we'll form a plan to save Ingrid."

Her stomach rumbled again as if it heard him mention food. She placed her hand in his and together, they headed up the curved staircase to his chamber.

Chapter 14

As they climbed the stairs, it truly sunk in they were headed to *his chamber*. She should have said no. She should have resisted. But the thought of someplace warm with warm food was much too appealing to turn down. And the way he held her hand and led her up the stairs with such care and concern gave her the heart squeeze.

At the top of the stairs, he turned left and headed down a long corridor with a soaring arched ceiling. There were guards stationed every few feet standing at rigid attention with their swords at their sides and their heads held high. As they passed, she tried to get a glimpse of them to see if they noticed them walking by, but none of them seemed to pay them any mind.

Along the walls, were more oil paintings. Some were likely family portraits of kings and queens of the past. Others were of lush green landscapes that seemed out of place with a winter wonderland outside.

They halted at a door on the left, which he pushed open and then stepped aside to allow her to enter.

This was more than a bed chamber. This was a suite. He had a sitting area with an oversized fireplace, the flickering flames jumping high into the chimney. Two sofas faced each other in front of the fireplace with a table in between. A plush garnet rug covered the stone floor. Candelabras were placed in every corner with every candle lit to illuminate the room in a bright, happy glow.

Bookshelves lined one wall. They were crammed full of books from top to bottom. Off the small living area was a round table with four chairs. A silver tea service sat in the middle and she fervently hoped there was hot tea inside. A closed door led to what she assumed was his bed chamber.

Nicholas stepped inside and closed the door behind him. He glanced around the large room. "I see they've already made some preparations."

He glanced around from the roaring fire to the lit candelabras. Even his private chamber was decked out in holiday decorations. A small tree perched in a corner adorned with twinkling lights flashing in a cheerful pattern. The mantle hosted greenery like the one in the great hall. A beautiful centerpiece with a hurricane glass hosted a flickering candle surrounded by green garland and sprigs of holly.

"You live here?" she asked, her voice more timid than she would have liked.

"I do. Can I take your cloak?" he asked.

She shrugged it off and handed it to him. He hung it on a peg near the door. She slid the sack off her shoulder, glad to be free of the weight of it. It had bounced against her hip the entire way, leaving it sore and achy.

He headed over to the table and poured two steaming mugs of tea. "How do you take it?"

"Cream and sugar," she said.

He added a dollop of cream and a bit of sugar and then brought her the porcelain cup. She smiled as she took it, grateful for the hot beverage.

"Let's sit by the fire while we wait for dinner." He motioned to the sofas near the fire.

She followed his lead and took the seat across from him, placing the sack with the slippers on the table and then perching on the edge of the cushion. Her nerves jangled as she took a sip of the tea.

"In the morning, I'll gather supplies and then we will ride for the mountains," he said. "The mountain pass up to her stronghold is rather difficult this time of year, so I hope you're prepared for that."

"I'll be ready," she said, taking another sip. The drink warmed her through, thawing her hands as she held the cup. She tipped her head to one side. "What do you mean by difficult?"

"I mean Malvina's keep is well guarded. She doesn't take kindly to visitors." He took a sip of tea and then placed the cup on the table, eyeing the bag with the shoes. "Are you still determined to go through with this rescue mission?"

She nodded without hesitation. "Yes, I am. We have to get Ingrid away from her. How are we going to get to her?"

"That's the big question, isn't it?" He sat back in the cushions and stared into the fire, a thoughtful expression on his face. "There will be no way to get through undetected. She'll know the moment we enter the pass. Likely, she'll capture us before we make it to the foot of the mountains."

Worry gnawed at her. "Then what?"

"Then we hope we can free ourselves long enough to find Ingrid and get out."

It sounded impossible. Ella dragged her lower lip through her teeth in contemplation as she held the cup in her hands. There had to be another way, but she wasn't versed in the geography of this world and so she didn't know if there was another way into the mountains.

A knock sounded on the door, interrupting her thoughts. Nicholas rose and opened the door to the servants who bustled in with a cart full of food. They went to work setting the table and moments later were gone.

He grinned at her from across the room. "Shall we dine?"

She placed her cup on the table next to his and headed for the table, taking a seat opposite him. There was roasted meat and vegetables in a brown gravy, cheese, bread, fruits, and more tea. She took small portions as she filled her plate while Nicholas heaped his.

"For a prince you have a hearty appetite," she said.

He laughed as he stuck a piece of meat with his fork. "It's been a while since the beef stew at the tavern."

She couldn't agree more as she took a bite of roasted meat. It was savory and practically melted in her mouth. They lapsed into silence as they both enjoyed the meal, but Ella could tell his mind was working to come up with a better plan.

He wiped his mouth with a cloth napkin. "Perhaps I'm thinking about this all wrong."

"What do you mean?" she asked.

He shoved back from the table and went to one of the bookshelves, his finger trailing down the spines until he found the one he wanted. It was a hefty tome as he pulled it off the shelf and carried it over to the table, dropping it with a thud. The dishes rattled. He flipped open the book and shuffled a few pages to the one he wanted and paused. It was two-page spread of a map of Rovenheim. She leaned in to get a better look as her heart picked up speed. It was almost as though he heard her thoughts about looking at a map.

He pointed to the mountain range northeast of the castle labeled Grimbrande near the coastline. "The pass through the mountains is here." He dragged his finger along what appeared to be a pathway through the middle of the mountains. "Her fortress is at the top of one of these mountains."

"But you said the mountain pass was guarded," she said.

He nodded. "And it will be difficult to get past the guards. But..." His voice trailed off as he swiped is hand over his smooth chin. "What if we took another road further north and approached the fortress from the south here?"

Ella rose from the chair and leaned over the map. "Is there a road there?"

"There used to be."

From what she could tell on the map, the fortress looked as though it backed against the coast. There was a tiny port town west of the fortress labeled Echo Harbor.

"This harbor here," she pointed to it. "Does it have ships?"

"Yes."

"That we can charter?"

Something twinkled deep in his eyes as he gave her a half smile. "Yes."

"Then why can't we charter a ship to take us near the coast where her fortress is. We can row a dingy to the coastline and then approach from the south like you mentioned. She would never know we were coming," Ella said.

"Why, Ella, that sounds positively brilliant." He beamed at her.

"Thank you."

She flushed hot at the compliment. It wasn't often she was complimented for her smarts. But then, she never had the opportunity to converse with someone like Nicholas.

"We will still need supplies and provisions. I'll gather them. We'll ride out tomorrow morning to Echo Harbor, though there may not be many ships there this time of year," he said.

"Why is that?"

"They tend to sail to warmer climates until winter passes. But there should still be a few in port."

Ella stifled a yawn as she placed her napkin by the side of her plate. Finally warm and with a full stomach, she was starting to feel drowsy.

"Oh, you must be exhausted. Let's get you to your chamber."

She had to admit that sounded lovely. She returned to the small seating area and picked up the bag with the slippers as he took her cloak from the peg by the door.

He extended an elbow to her, a warm smile lighting up his face as he offered to escort her. His eyes sparkled with affection and happiness, filling her heart with warmth and joy. She took his arm.

He pulled open the door and led her out into the hallway. The guards were still stationed every few feet and still did not give her a second glance. They walked down the length of the hallway to the last door where he paused.

"Here we are."

"This is the west wing," she said, recalling the earlier conversation with Magnus.

"It is."

"And my room in next to yours?" Her voice quivered a little at the thought of being so close to him.

"I hope that's all right with you," he said. "It seemed the best choice. The guest chambers are in the east wing. But I know you're in a strange place and I didn't want you to feel as though I abandoned you."

Her throat tightened as warmth expanded through her chest. It had been so long since anyone had thought of her needs, she wasn't quite sure how to react.

"That was so thoughtful of you." Her voice only trembled a little when she spoke.

He handed her the cloak, then pushed open the door, remaining in the hallway as she moved to step inside. He placed a hand on her arm and she paused, turning to him.

"Pleasant dreams, Ella." He kissed her on the cheek.

And then he was gone. Heading back down the hallway to his own room.

Ella stood rooted in place as she watched him go, lifting her hand to her cheek where he kissed her. It was merely a peck. Certainly nothing to feel gushy about, but he had kissed her nonetheless. Her heart thudded hard in her chest as she stepped inside the room and pushed the door closed.

Her chamber was as big as his and almost identical in layout. She, too, had a small seating area by an enormous fireplace that hosted a lovely warming blaze. She, too, had a table and chairs in an adjacent dining area. She didn't have the bookshelves he had, though. It was also decorated as his was with the small tree in the corner, the greenery on the mantle, and the centerpiece on the dining table.

She wandered into the sitting area, dropping her cloak on one of the chairs as she stood before the fire, letting the warmth of it cascade through her. What a wonderous and beautiful place the castle was and how lucky Nicholas was to live here. To never have to worry about his next meal or if he were going to be ordered around by a hateful shrew and her two spoiled daughters. She was rather envious of that life, but then, he was a prince, after all. He was used to this kind of life, just as she was used to the one she had.

One she would, eventually, have to return to. Her gut twisted into a knot at the thought of returning to her stepmother and stepsisters.

A swift knock on her door startled her. "Yes?"

The door pushed open and an older woman popped her head in. "Ah, here you are, my lady. We've brought up a copper tub for your bath."

"Oh!" she said on a breath.

Before she could wave them off, the woman pushed the door open to allow the men inside carrying the tub. They passed through the living area and through a door that she assumed was her private bed chamber. Several maids followed with steaming kettles. None of them gave her so much as a glance as they headed into the room. Moments later, the men exited and the maids came out with empty kettles.

The woman waved her toward the room. "Come and I'll help you."

"Oh, I appreciate that but I think I can manage on my own."

She tipped her head to one side but didn't argue. "As you wish, my lady."

They all filed out, closing the door behind them.

Ella took a tentative step toward the bedroom and halted in the doorway. There were several candelabras lit and blazing, a fireplace across from the giant four-poster bed. In front of the fireplace, the copper tub they delivered full of steaming water.

Grinning broadly, Ella placed the bag with the slippers on the bed. She noticed, then, there was a stack of plush towels and next to it a thick nightgown. She stripped and stepped into the warm water, allowing it to seep into her tired muscles.

After she bathed, toweled off and dressed, she climbed into the bed with the thick quilts, soft sheets, and plush pillows. She had never experienced such luxury.

The sack with the slippers were still on the bed. She pulled it over to her and took out the shoes one at a time. Then she placed them on the night table next to the bed, watching as the firelight flickered and danced over the facets of glass, giving them a rainbow iridescence. They were so beautiful, so delicate, so perfect.

She dropped the sack on the floor next to the bed and burrowed down under the covers, pulling them up to her chin. Her eyes were heavy as she watched the fire flickering orange, red, and yellow flames upward.

As she drifted off, she thought she saw a flash of light from the slippers, as though they twinkled with joy at finally be released from the captivity of the sack. But then she decided it was nothing more than her tired mind and her imagination playing tricks on her. Moments later, she was fast asleep.

CHAPTER 15

Malvina's attempts to bring the glass slippers to her had failed. She thought stealing the girl from the village would push those useless villagers into action. But no. Though she threatened to take another, she really didn't have the desire to have another pathetic hostage in her care.

At least their Christmas Star was destroyed now, plunging the happy little village into quiet despair. She'd sensed that the moment it shattered. She paused, remembering the tinkling of glass when it cracked and stifled a laugh.

It had been so satisfying seeing that smashed into pieces.

But she still had the issue of the missing glass slippers. She *needed* them if she was going to remove Noella from her throne and take over the realm of Rovenheim. Those slippers had the power to manipulate feelings and she wanted them.

Thinking of Noella sent the ire rising through her. Her face flushed hot as she thought of the woman who stole them out from under her. How dare she.

She paced her bedchamber, her hands clenching and unclenching into fists. How did the slippers get past her in the village? Who had them? And how were they able to conceal them? She knew they were there. She'd sensed their magic.

She halted her pacing and went to the tapestry concealing the Dark Mirror, shoving it aside.

"Dark Mirror, tell me what I seek. Where are the glass slippers?"

The mirror's face appeared inside the smokey circle. "The young woman still has them, my beautiful and desperate queen."

Fisting her hands, she said, "Where is she?"

There was a long pause before the mirror answered. "She is no longer in the village."

When the mirror didn't elaborate, she huffed out a heated breath. "Then *where* is she?"

"She comes to your keep, my dark and dangerous queen." Another pause. "With the prince."

"The prince?"

She tapped her forefinger against her chin as she resumed her pacing. "There is only one reason why the crown prince would come here. Perhaps he thinks to rescue my prisoner. And if the young woman is with him and she carries the slippers..." A laugh bubbled up her throat. "Well, then. I shall have them at last."

"And the crown prince," the mirror added.

"Ha! Yes, and the crown prince. Noella will have no choice but to bend the knee to me. And then...I shall rule all of Rovenheim. I must prepare."

She covered the mirror once again and then hurried out to make sure her prisoner was secured.

A knocking on her door awoke her from a deep sleep. She sat upright in bed, trying to remember where she was as her surroundings were momentarily unfamiliar. Then it all came rushing back to her. Nicholas, the prince, bringing her to his castle, feeding her a delicious meal, and then taking her to her own private chamber where she had a luxurious bath and slept in the coziest bed.

The fire was now nothing more than embers and there was a chill in the room. She was reluctant to leave her snug nest.

"Rise and shine, my lady!" It was the older lady who had returned. She burst into the bedroom with an armload of clothes which she dumped on the end. She gave her a bright smile. "Did you sleep well?"

"Yes, very well, thank you." Ella pushed aside the covers. When her bare feet hit the cold floor, a shiver went up her spine.

"His highness asked me to bring you some warmer clothes for your travels." She waved to the mound on the bed. "Let's get you dressed—oh!" She gasped when she saw the glass slippers on the table by the bed. She bustled over, leaning down to get a good look at them. "Those are lovely."

Ella bent to pick up the sack that had fallen on the floor. She reached for one of the shoes, holding it up for the woman to see.

"They're made of glass!" she said, her eyes alight with excitement.

Ella couldn't hide her smile at the woman's delight. "They are."

She peered at them longingly. "There's a legend about a pair of glass slippers. Have you heard it?"

Ella shook her head.

"It is said they can only be worn by the person they're meant for, they make the wearer dance with beauty and grace, and can lead the wearer to her true love!"

Her heart did a tumble in her chest. Is that why her fairy godmother had gifted them to her? Because she knew they would, ultimately, lead her to Nicholas?

The woman leaned closer, dropping her voice to a whisper. "It's also said they're connected to the emotions of the wearer."

She blinked, staring at the woman in shocked silence. Was that why Malvina wanted them so desperately? To use them to manipulate others?

"It is true?" Ella asked, her voice a whisper.

"Legends rarely are, dear." The woman waved away the tale as if it were nothing but a silly myth. "Listen to me going on and on when we need to get you dressed. Your prince is waiting."

A hot blush crawled up her neck. "Oh, he's not my prince."

"Oh?" She lifted one gray brow. "Seems to me he's taking a liking to you, my dear."

"How do you mean?" Ella clutched the slipper so tight, her hand cramped.

"He gave you one of the royal suites." She waved a hand to encompass their surroundings.

The *royal* suite. Her heart did a wild dance as she tried to make sense of that.

"Come on, now. Let's get you dressed."

She reached for the slipper to take it out of Ella's hand but she held it closer to her chest and shook her head. The woman pulled her hand back with a bemused look on her face.

"Just where did you get those slippers?"

"They were a gift from someone." She almost said her fairy godmother but then she thought better of it. She placed the one she held inside the sack, then reached for the other one.

"It seems to me you need something better to carry them in," the woman said as she eyed her.

"I don't have anything else."

A thoughtful look crossed her face. "Let's get you dressed and then I'll see what I can find."

A few minutes later, the woman—who's name she learned was Alice—had her dressed in layers that would surely keep her warm. Stockings, an underdress, a wool overdress and her boots. She'd add the final layer—the cloak Agnes gave her—when they left.

Alice had bustled out of her room and returned moments later with a small red velvet bag with a long drawstring. Ella transferred the slippers to the new bag. They were a perfect fit. Alice took the old flour sack with her tattered servant's gown still in it.

"Will you be needing this anymore?" she asked as she held it up.

Ella thought about that for a moment as she considered whether or not she would ever wear that gown again. At last, she shook her head. "I won't."

"I'll take care of it for you."

And by that, Ella assumed she would dispose of it along with the gown.

"Now, let's get you to the prince."

She motioned for Ella to follow her. At the door, Ella paused to grab her cloak. They headed out of the royal suite—she was still stunned by that—and down the long hallway where Nicholas waited. He wore traveling clothes that were much like hers. Thick pants, boots, a thick long-sleeved tunic under a leather vest. A sword was strapped to one side, a dagger to the other. His cloak was over one arm. He gave her a warm smile when he saw her. It was clear he was happy to see her.

"Good morning!" He eyed the velvet bag. "What's that?"

"The slippers," she said, still clutching the bag to her.

"You could leave them here for safe keeping."

Elle shook her head. "I'll carry them."

"I don't think you'll be getting her to part with them, your highness," Alice said with a chuckle. Then she dipped a quick curtsy. "Safe travels and Godspeed to you both."

With that, she was off down the hallway, leaving them alone.

"I only suggested it because of where we're going," he said.

She slipped the long drawstring over her shoulder and tucked the bag under her arm. "I would feel better keeping it on me."

She was tempted to wear them, but then wearing glass slippers in the snow wasn't practical.

"All right, then." He held his arm out to her. "Shall we? Breakfast is waiting in the great hall."

Her stomach rumbled at the thought. It had been a while since she'd had regular meals. The last time was before she was made to be a servant in her own home, when her father was still around and her stepmother wasn't such a witch.

They walked down the curved staircase to the great hall where the fire was still blazing brightly in the oversized hearth, keeping the room warm. They feasted on thick porridge and oat cakes and washed it down with delicious hot tea.

As they finished, she wrapped her cloak around her shoulders. Magnus bustled in, wringing his hands. Worry lines creased his forehead.

"My prince, are you certain this is the best course of action?"

"Yes, Magnus. Have you the provisions I asked for?" He took Ella by the hand and led her out of the great hall, down a long corridor.

Magnus hurried to keep up, his breath labored with Nicholas's quick steps. "Of course, they're ready, but—"

"Are the horses saddled and packed?" Nicholas asked, cutting him off.

"Yes, your highness, but—"

"Good. Then we shall be on our way."

"I really must protest," Magnus said, trying again. "What if something should happen to you?"

Nicholas paused, still holding her hand, and turned to his steward. "I'll be fine. We have a plan for getting into the fortress."

Magnus's eyes narrowed. "But do you have a plan for getting the girl and getting out?"

He pressed his lips together in a thin line. "Not exactly but I'm working on it."

"Your highness, with the king and queen away, I simply must protest. My job is to make sure you are safe and this kingdom is safe. Seeing you run off to the Grimbrande Mountains seems like folly."

Nicholas released her hand and took a step toward the steward. He put a hand on his shoulder. "Don't worry, Magnus. I promise you we'll make it back in one piece *and* with the girl from the village."

He said nothing for a long moment as he pressed his lips together. "And what shall I tell your mother should she return and ask after you?"

Nicholas cut a sheepish glance at Ella, then said, "Tell her not to worry."

And with that, they were off.

He led her through the massive castle to the stables where two saddled horses waited for them along with one of the stable hands. Another man stood in front of the horses with his hands clasped in front of him, a fur-lined cloak around his shoulders to ward off the cold wintry air. He was tall, with a bearded face, crinkles at the corner of his eyes, and piercing dark brown eyes.

"Hello, Gustav," Nicholas said as they approached. "Have you come to see us off?"

He scowled. "No, your highness. I intend to accompany you."

Nicholas halted, his hand squeezing hers as Gustav cut a glance at her and gave her a good once-over, question deep in his eyes.

"You're not coming with us." Nicholas released her hand and headed for his horse.

She took a tentative step toward the other horse, watching to see what was going to happen next. Gustav moved to stand in front of Nicholas, blocking his path to the horse.

"I'm afraid I can't let you go alone," he said.

They had a long, silent staring competition.

"I can take care of myself," Nicholas said.

Then Gustav nodded toward her with question creasing his face. "And what about her?"

"What about her?" Nicholas asked. "I can take care of her, too."

Ella stepped forward, extending her hand. "I'm Ella, by the way."

He was surprised by her sudden introduction and hesitated a moment before taking her hand in his. "Gustav. I'm Captain of the Guard. It's a pleasure to meet you, my lady." He cut a glance to Nicholas. "And I'm coming with you no matter what you say."

"Because you think it will be dangerous?" Ella asked.

"Because I know it will be dangerous," he said.

"Then perhaps you should accompany us." She walked around to her horse, stuck her foot in the stirrup and swung herself up into the saddle.

Nicholas gaped at her. Gustav did the same.

"Well, then, I guess you're going with us," Nicholas said then.

"As I should." Gustav said with a nod.

Ella clutched the reins in her gloved hands and sat tall in the saddle, trying to decide how she felt about a great many things. First, about everyone calling her *my lady* when she certainly was not. Second, about Gustav coming with them on their trek to the Grimbrande Mountains to rescue Ingrid. While she thought it was a good idea, she much enjoyed Nicholas's company and was looking forward to spending more time with him.

Gustav, it seemed, had anticipated the upcoming trip and already had a horse saddled and ready. When they were both seated and ready, Nicholas gave a quick nod.

"Well, then, let's be on our way."

Nicholas kicked his horse into a gallop and headed out of the stable. Gustav gave her a grin and motioned for her to go next.

"After you, my lady."

She followed Nicholas, nudging her horse into a gallop. Gustav followed her, bringing up the rear.

And as they left the stable and the safety of Rovenheim castle, her gut clenched. She was on a new adventure with two men she hardly knew. What would her father think?

Alternatively, what would her stepmother think? She stifled a giggle at the thought of her stepmother's horror-stricken look at the idea Ella was headed toward a place she had never seen to rescue a girl she had never met.

She was actually going on the adventure she had always dreamed of instead of cleaning chamber pots, cooking meals for the ungrateful, cleaning until her hands were raw, as well as doing all the mending and the sewing and taking care of all the animals while the three of them loafed around the manor. It made her heart smile and sent a thrill of excitement through her.

She sat a little taller in the saddle, clutched the reins a little tighter, and felt her confidence soar as they headed toward the port.

CHAPTER 16

"So, Ella, tell me how you came to be in the company of our rogue prince?" Gustav asked as they trotted along toward the port.

She cut Nicholas a glance whose mouth had formed into a thin line. "I am not a rogue prince."

Gustav laughed. "How many lady friends did you entertain this summer?"

The prince's face flushed a deep red. "Don't listen to him, Ella. He's merely trying to cause trouble."

"And you don't?" Gustav countered.

Ella glanced between the two of them. Gustav had a smirk on his face while Nicholas was less than amused. While she had no right to the prince—they hardly knew each other after all—a pang of jealousy went through her anyway.

"You entertained lady friends?" she asked, one brow raised.

"They were merely acquaintances," Nicholas said. Then he said to Gustav, "Ella and I met at a royal ball."

"Indeed?" But there was more question in his eyes.

Clearly, he wanted to find out more about how they met, but Nicholas wasn't so ready to divulge that information. Ella wasn't sure if she should tell Gustav the truth, either. After all, it sounded odd to say she had arrived by the magical glass slippers. She wasn't sure the Captain of the Guard would believe her.

All of that seemed like a terribly long time ago, now.

"Yes," she said. "At a royal ball."

"Was that something your mother arranged?"

Nicholas gave him a pointed look as they rode along. "You're not helping."

Yet, Nicholas didn't deny his mother had something to do with it.

"His mother has a way with making things happen," Gustav said to her, a twinkle in his dark brown eyes.

"I haven't met his mother," she said.

"You haven't?" Gustav said.

Nicholas cleared his throat loudly. "No, not yet." Again, he gave him a pointed look.

"Well," Gustav said on a breath, "I'm sure she will in good time."

"I'm sure she will," Nicholas agreed.

"I've known Nicholas all my life," he said, changing the subject. "We grew up together. Have you known the prince long, my lady?"

She glanced at the prince whose face was still bright red. He wasn't enjoying Gustav's company at all.

"Not long," she said shaking her head.

"And...are you visiting Rovenheim?"

"I think that's quite enough with the questions," Nicholas said. "We're almost to the port. Let's make haste."

With that, he kicked his horse into a gallop and headed off, snow spraying in his wake.

"I guess I made him angry," Gustav said, giving her a sheepish grin.

"I guess you did," she said with a nod.

They followed Nicholas's lead and hurried after him.

The rest of the trip was silent and uneventful. Until they arrived at the port. They dismounted their horses and left them with a boarder while they sought a suitable ship. The fierce wind whipped through Ella and she pulled her cloak tighter around her thin frame. The hood refused to stay on her head, so her ears and face were nearly frozen as they walked down the wharf.

There were only two ships in the harbor. One was a merchant ship with only a few sailors aboard. The captain was on shore leave and, therefore, they weren't planning to leave the port until spring. The few men aboard were only there to keep things tidy and make sure nothing happened to the ship while it was in port.

The second ship was one with several masts soaring into the overcast sky. The sails were all put away, but there were several boisterous men aboard. One hung on the railing as they approached. His overcoat was shabby. He wore fingerless gloves, no hat, and several layers under the coat. His bearded face was smudged with dirt and his long hair was unruly in the wind. Ella had never met a pirate and had only imagined what one looked like. This man looked like a pirate to her.

She shifted from one foot to the other, the velvet bag under her arm shifting, too. She had forgotten it was there while riding and now the slight weight of it reminded her she still carried the glass slippers.

"Ahoy, there!" he called with a wave. "It's not often we see visitors on the wharf this time of year."

"Hello," Nicholas said with a smile. His face was pink from the cold wind. "We're looking for passage to the Grimbrande Mountains."

"The Grimbrande?" He scratched his scraggly gray beard. "There's no port near those mountains."

"I was hoping you could sail us close and then let us take one of your dinghies to shore," Nicholas said.

"*That's* your plan?" Gustav asked under his breath. "You didn't tell me that."

"It wasn't relevant," Nicholas said, his voice low so the pirate wouldn't hear.

Gustav frowned, clearly unhappy with the proposed plan.

"And then what? Wait it out in the waters until you return?" the pirate asked and then emitted a jolly laugh.

"I'll pay you," Nicholas said.

That seemed to get his attention. He stopped laughing, leaned over the railing further and narrowed his eyes. "How much?"

"How much do you want?" Nicholas said.

Astonishment flickered through Ella as she looked from the prince to the pirate.

"Five hundred gold," the pirate said.

Without blinking an eye, Nicholas said, "Deal. And we leave now."

The pirate was unphased by the prince's demands, turned and shouted to the crew, "Lower the sails, me lads, we're setting sail!"

It didn't take long for the crusty old pirate to get the ship ready to sail. He was momentarily leery of allowing a woman on board, but Nicholas talked him into it, telling him he simply couldn't leave his sister behind. Ella tried hard not to roll her eyes at that.

Once they were on board, Gustav took Nicholas aside and they had heated words. Ella remained at the railing watching as the ship pulled out from the port, trying her best to keep her ears to herself. She shivered against the chilly breeze and pulled her hood up over her face to block out as much of the wind as possible. It didn't help much.

When Gustav and Nicholas were finished arguing, Nicholas then spoke with the pirate, which she assumed was the captain.

"Here is half now," he said as he handed over a small draw-string bag. "The rest when we return safely to port."

"You drive a hard bargain, sir."

Sir. So, Nicholas hadn't told him his true identity.

When he finished with the pirate, he joined her at the railing. He leaned on his forearms, the wind gusting past his face. She watched the distance expand between the ship and the port, her heart a wild beat of both excitement and fear. And a bit of nerves and anger as he stood next to her as if nothing was amiss.

"The captain says we will be there shortly. Then we'll take a rowboat out to the shore," he said.

She nodded.

He leaned in closer and dropped his voice. "He's a crusty old thing, but I trust him. Name's Captain Bart, short for Bartholemew."

She nodded again. He turned serious.

"Are you angry with me?"

Was she? She didn't really have an answer to that question. Since Gustav mentioned all his lady friends, she hadn't been able to stop thinking about it. She had no idea why it bothered her so much, either. It wasn't like the prince had made her any promises.

"Your friend, Gustav, is an interesting person," she said, keeping her face forward.

"Gustav likes to tease me," he said. "That's all."

She turned her head to look at him, but the edge of her hood blocked out most of his face. "Why *were* you at that ball?" she asked suddenly. She didn't know why that question seemed so important for him to answer now.

But she also thought of what Alice told her. That the magic in the glass slippers would lead the wearer to her true love.

He kept his face forward, the wind tousling his hair. "I was there as a guest, like you."

Then he turned to her, taking her gloved hands in his and squeezing. "You mustn't take Gustav seriously with all those things he said about the ball and my mother arranging it. I was there and we met. I'm glad we met, Ella."

"And then you came to Rovenheim to find me," she said. "Why? How did you know I was here?"

He was quiet for a long moment, indecision in his eyes as he decided how to answer. "Ella, you must believe me there are some things that cannot be explained. I came to find you, yes, and to make sure you were returned safely to your own world."

She slipped her hands free and turned back to the railing. The wharf had diminished in size.

"My own world." She hadn't meant to sound so bitter.

"Don't you want to return?"

Ella thought about that for a long, quiet moment. What did she really have to go back to? Her parents were dead. Her stepmother and stepsisters were vile. They treated her like she was nothing more than dirt on the bottom of their shoes. She did wonder, however, how they were faring in her absence. If they had figured out how to cook and clean and take care of the livestock. She thought of one of her stepsisters mucking stalls almost made her laugh.

But then Nicholas had made her no promises, so what kind of life would she have if she stayed?

"I have nothing to go back to," she said at last.

"No family?" he asked.

"My mother died when I was young," she said. "My father left for a business trip a few years ago and never returned. I was left to contend with my stepmother and stepsisters."

She tried to hide her disgust for them, but it was difficult.

"You don't get along with them?" he guessed.

A half-hearted laugh escaped her before she could stop it. "Not exactly."

She refused to tell him how they treated her. She didn't want to admit such things. And, as he was keen to say, it wasn't relevant. Not to him.

"But..." she paused, thinking of their manor and all the Christmas decorations she left behind in her room, all the festive cheer from the patrons in the market. "I do miss some things."

Nicholas turned toward her, leaning an elbow on the railing and giving her his full attention. "Like?"

"Like the cheer in the marketplace during this time of year. How everyone seems joyful for no reason other than the season. My stepmother wouldn't let me put a tree up in the foyer. So, I put it up in my room."

"Your stepmother sounds like a shrew," he said then.

It made her laugh. "But that's enough about them. What are we going to do when we arrive at the shore?"

He straightened, smoothing his gloved hands over the front of his cloak. "We are going to hike through the mountains to her fortress and hope she doesn't know we're coming."

"That doesn't sound reassuring," she said.

"No, and it's not Gustav's favorite idea, either. But it's the only plan we have."

A plan she helped concoct.

"Then I suppose it will have to do."

He nodded and turned his attention back out to sea. Though he sounded confident, she sensed his apprehension. She had to admit, she felt exactly the same.

CHAPTER 17

True to his word, the pirate captain got them close enough to the shoreline to allow them to row the rest of the way. Nicholas promised extra gold to the captain if the ship was still waiting for them when they returned. Ella sat in the middle. Nicholas was in front of her, Gustav behind her and each of them had a set of oars as they rowed to the shore.

Here on the water, the wind was brutal. She pulled her hood down tight and clutched her elbows, the velvet bag digging into her side. The black, snow-capped mountains soared into the late afternoon sky so high she had to crane her neck to look up at them. At the top, she made out the outline of the dark queen's fortress.

An overwhelming sense of foreboding came over her. Perhaps this wasn't such a good idea after all.

As they neared the shore, Nicholas hopped out in ankle deep water. Gustav did the same. They pulled up the boat onto the damp sand. Nicholas held his hand out to her, helping her step over the edge. They all paused there, looking upward at the fortress. Ella's heart rammed in her chest, her anxiety level high.

"Well, here goes nothing," Gustav said. "Stay behind me."

"Why?" Nicholas demanded.

He gave him a cutting glance. "So, I can protect you and Ella if anything happens."

Nicholas merely nodded. He took her by the hand as they fell in step behind the Captain of the Guard. Their footsteps left deep indentations in the wet sand as they headed down the beach toward the craggy section of the mountains. As the sun dipped closer to the horizon, deep shadows cast along the beach and through the mountain pass.

The suffocating darkness enveloped them as they ventured deeper into the foreboding crevice. Jagged rocks jutted out from the ground, casting eerie silhouettes that seemed to taunt and threaten their existence.

On either side of them, the mountains soared upward, blotting out the sky which was quickly turning from pale blue to deep indigo. Ella clutched Nicholas's hand tighter and as they followed Gustav, their shoulders brushed. Gustav had his sword at the ready, for whatever good that might do.

"Do you know where you're going?" Nicholas said, his voice a quiet whisper, as if speaking louder would disturb their surroundings.

"I have a general idea," Gustav replied, his voice just as quiet. "Malvina is dangerous so we need to be on our guard."

"But she doesn't know we're coming," Nicholas said.

"I wouldn't count on that," he replied.

A shudder went through Ella as the darkness closed in. She had never been one for being outside in the dark and she didn't like it now. She edged closer to Nicholas.

"Are you all right?" he asked, his voice low.

She nodded, giving him her best reassuring smile.

Ahead, the path widened, giving them more room to walk. A sense of relief passed through her as she glanced upward to the night sky. Twinkling stars appeared, but these weren't familiar constellations. At the top of the mountain, she thought she saw movement. Like a dark figure that had moved from the edge. It was hard to tell, though, in the deepening twilight.

She stared at the top of the mountains as they continued. She was certain she saw the figure again. And then another. And another.

"Nicholas—"

But as she tried to shout the warning, arrows landed all around them just missing each of them by inches.

"Run!" Gustav ordered.

The three of them took off at a run down the mountain path, heading for another crevice. More arrows rained down around them. Nicholas's hand tightened on hers as they sprinted over rocks and uneven ground. Then Gustav went down with a shout. He dropped his sword as he crashed against the ground, holding his leg.

Nicholas released her hand and unsheathed his sword. He held it aloft and murmured something she couldn't hear. The sword lit up and a blast of bright white light shot out from it toward the top of the mountain.

She halted, shocked and in awe. His sword was...magic? No, that was impossible.

Gustav dragged his body toward one of the craggy rocks. An arrow stuck out of his leg just above his knee. He grimaced with the pain as Nicholas reached him. He wrapped his arm around his friend's waist and hoisted him to his feet.

"Leave me," Gustav said with a groan.

"We need to get to the crevice. Ella, grab his sword."

She hoisted it up, surprised at the weight of it as she hurried after them. Gustav hobbled, favoring his injured leg, while Nicholas shouldered most of his weight. They made it to the crevice and were once again shrouded by the safety of the soaring mountains.

Nicholas halted, lowering Gustav to the outcropping of rock. He rested against it, his face contorted in pain. Ella leaned his sword against the rock next to him. Nicholas sheathed his sword and then inspected his wound.

"Hard to see in the dark," he said. "It missed your knee."

"Well, that's good news," Gustav said through gritted teeth. "They waited until we were in the open to attack. She knows you're here, Nick."

His lips thinned as he clenched his jaw, his muscles flexing there. "I know but I'm not turning back now."

Gustav grasped him by the upper arm and jerked him close. "You're that determined?"

He cut a glance at Ella, then said, "I am."

Gustav groaned. "Fine. Then follow this path. At the end, turn left. You'll see a staircase carved into the side of the mountain. That will lead you to her fortress. But Nick—" He paused, gritting his teeth against the pain, "I think you should turn back."

"I'm not turning back. We've come too far." Nicholas glanced down at the arrow sticking out of his leg. "It doesn't look too deep. I can break it off and wrap it up so you won't bleed to death. The healer can remove the point when we get back to Rovenheim."

"You're going to leave him here?" Ella asked, unable to hide her astonishment.

"No," Gustav said. "I'm going to drag myself back to the row boat."

"And then what?" she demanded, her hands on her hips. She had forgotten all about the cold wind and her fear of the dark.

"I'll row back to the ship and see if I can get reinforcements from Captain Bart," he said.

"It'll take you considerable time to get back there," Nicholas said. "And there are likely still archers out there." He nodded behind them at the crevice.

"That's a chance I'll have to take. If I go now, while it's dark, I should be able to make it."

Nicholas nodded. He reached into his cloak and ripped out the lining, handing her the shredded cloth. Then he reached for the arrow, wrapping his hand around the wooden shaft.

"Make it quick," Gustav said.

As he nodded, he snapped it in two as close to his leg as possible. There was only a small piece sticking out. Ella handed Nicholas the cloth. He wrapped it around his friend's leg and tied a secure knot.

"Go on," Gustav said. "I'll wait until you're out of sight before I make a break for it." He wrapped his hand around the hilt of his sword.

"Good luck," he said.

"And to you both," Gustav replied with a nod.

Nicholas reached for her hand again. "Are you ready?"

She took a deep breath, expelled it. "As I'll ever be."

And though she sounded confident, her nerves jangled. They said farewell to Gustav and started down the path the direction he told them to go.

"Will he be all right?" she asked as they made their way through the frigid night.

"He'll be fine. He can take care of himself."

"But you're not worried about him?" she asked.

"Gustav is tough and resilient. I have no doubt he'll make it back to the ship," he said, flashing her a reassuring grin.

They walked on in silence, but she couldn't stop thinking about what he did with his sword. It was almost as though he had used magic to make it flash bright like that, but then, that seemed silly.

"Your sword lit up." She hadn't meant to blurt the words, but they came out.

His head snapped in her direction. "My sword?"

"Yes. Your sword. It blinded the archers, didn't it?"

"It did," he admitted.

"But how?" she asked.

A mischievous glint danced in his eyes as he playfully flashed a grin. "Magic," was his only reply.

He looked straight ahead, squinting in the darkness as if that would help him see better. They were coming to the end of the path and he turned left and halted. Ella stopped next to him and peered toward the crude staircase carved in the side of the mountain, her heart beating at a rapid pace.

"He was right," he breathed, as if he wasn't sure Gustav had told them the truth.

"You doubted him?" she asked.

"It's not that I doubted him..." he paused, running a hand over his chin. "It's just that..."

"You doubted him," she finished.

"I may have doubted him a little. It's just that I don't know how he knew this was here."

She tipped her head back to look up at the staircase that seemed to be enveloped by the shadowy darkness.

"This will lead us to her fortress?" she asked.

He looked back at her, but it was hard to see his expression in the gloom. His eyes were nothing more than black orbs. "Let's find out, shall we?"

CHAPTER 18

Ella started to climb the steps first, Nicholas behind her. The steps were just wide enough for her foot and steep. It wasn't long before her legs started to burn from the exertion. She kept her attention focused on the next stair in front of her and then the next and the next so she wouldn't think about how far up they were going.

"How are you doing?" he asked, with a grunt.

"Great," she said, trying to sound as if she meant it.

He chuckled.

"How about you?"

Here the steps widened and became more straight up than at an angle of a regular staircase. She reached up, looking for a handhold to hoist herself up.

"I'm great, too," he said, though he didn't sound like he believed it.

She made the grave error of looking up. Her stomach clenched at the sight above her. The staircase seemed to go on forever. She paused, her arms and legs shaking. The wind whipped through them the higher they went.

"I'm not sure about this, Nicholas," she said, her voice strained with fear.

"You can do this," he said, reassuring her.

For the moment, she was paralyzed with anxiety.

"Just take it one step at a time," he said.

She reached for the next handhold, grabbed onto the edge of the stair, then pulled herself up.

"That's it," he said, cheering her on from below.

Then she made the mistake of looking down. The ground was far below, the wind whipping through them. She sucked in a sharp breath as she realized it was just as far to go down as it was to continue going up.

"Don't look at the ground, Ella," he said.

"I can't do this." Her voice was nothing but a roughened whisper.

"You *can*. Ella, look at me." He moved upward a step, closing the short gap between them. His face was right on her heels. "Look at me, Ella."

Her attention drifted from the ground to his upturned face and met his glittering blue, soulful eyes. There was comfort there.

"I'm right behind you."

She knew he was, but he was trying to give her courage. "I'm scared."

"I know you are, but you're doing great," he reassured.

"We're almost to the top."

"And then we find Ingrid," he said. "And go home."

"Home?" Her brows drew together in question.

"Yes, home. To Rovenheim," he said. "And when we return, you can have a long hot bath and sleep for as long as you like."

"In your castle?"

He nodded. "In my castle. In the room next to mine."

It sounded like a permanent invitation but she knew better than to hope for such a thing. Rovenheim was his home, not hers.

She turned back to the rock in front of her, reached for the next step and pulled herself up. Her gloves were starting to wear from constantly grabbing the rockface. Her legs burned. Her arms throbbed. Her hands ached. But somehow, she managed to keep going. Step after step. Until at last, she could see the top. Hope rose in her breast. She wanted to hurry, but she knew if she did, she could make a fatal mistake. So, she took those steps slowly until finally she reached the top of the mountain.

When she made it to the final stair, she dragged her tired body across it. She scurried away from the edge and then leaned over on her hands and knees to see if he needed help. He reached up for her. She grasped his hand and though he didn't need the help, he accepted her assistance. He practically crawled from the last stair and then rolled to his back, laying there a long moment to catch his breath as he looked up into the night sky. As his chest rose and fell with his deep breaths, white plumes fogged around his face.

It was colder up here than on the ground. She shivered even under the thick layers of clothing. And then she recalled the velvet bag. She pulled it out from under her cloak and opened the drawstring to peer inside it. The shoes were still there and fully intact.

Relief sputtered through her.

Nicholas was probably right in that she should have left them behind at the castle for safekeeping, but she felt as though it was the wrong thing to do. That she should keep them on her person at all times. Something about them pulled at her. Noella had entrusted her with them, after all. Leaving them behind seemed dangerous.

But then, bringing them to the queen's fortress could prove even more dangerous.

"That was...quite a climb," he puffed out.

She closed up the drawstring bag and slid it back under her cloak. "It was."

Now, sitting on the cold mountaintop, she glanced around but saw nothing but the shadowy shapes of more rocks and patches of snow.

How long had it taken them to climb that steep staircase?

Finally, Nicholas sat up and ran a gloved hand through his hair. Though he was closer to her, she had a difficult time making out his features in the inky blackness.

"Now what?" she asked.

"The fortress can't be far now," he said. He got to his feet. "Stay here."

"Where are you going?" Fear pounded through her at the thought of being left alone on the mountaintop.

"I'm going over there." He pointed ahead of him. "It looks like there might be a small cave on the side of the mountain. Or at least an opening. I'll be right back."

She drew her knees up to her chest and watched him walk away, his form turning into a shadow and blending in with the rest of the gloom. She stared in the space he had occupied only moments ago, straining her eyes as she watched for his shape to return to her. Long, cold moments passed and he didn't return.

Her heart plummeted to her stomach. She pushed to her feet, her tired body protesting.

"Nicholas?" she called.

There was no answer.

She moved away from the edge of the mountaintop trying to ignore it and her fear of tumbling over it to her death.

"Where are you?" she called again.

Again, the only answer was that of the wind whipping through her and whistling over the rock. She took a tentative step and then another toward the place he had seemingly disappeared into with her heart in her throat. She envisioned all sorts of terrible things happening to him. Like being captured by the queen's men or attacked by some silent, shadowy creature.

"Nicholas?" she called again, this time louder as she made her way closer to what he suggested was a small cave.

Indeed, it did look to be a narrow opening in the rock. But did she dare go inside there? She clutched her elbows, hugging herself tight. Her legs trembled as she forced herself to take another tentative step. The darkness seemed to close in around her like a suffocating shroud, amplifying the sense of impending danger. A cold sweat broke out across her brow as a chill ran down her spine, sending shivers through her. She couldn't tear her eyes away from that foreboding spot ahead.

Suddenly, a form burst from the small opening. She cried out, a sharp gasp escaping her lips. Her heart thundered in her ears. Then she realized it was Nicholas and blew out a breath. It plumed around her frozen face. He skidded to a halt when he saw her.

"Ella!" He hurried to her gripping her by the shoulders. "You won't believe it. Come."

"What is it? What did you find?"

He wrapped an arm around her. "Watch your step. The ground is uneven at first, but then smooths out."

He clutched her to him, helping her navigate the rocky terrain. She stared down at her feet as they walked. She stumbled once, but his strong form was there to keep her steady. He was also right that the ground smoothed out, as though someone had spent an inordinate amount of time on their hands and knees polishing the ground until it was perfect.

"Ella, look." His voice was nothing but a whisper.

She looked ahead and saw the path had indeed smoothed out and was as though it were man-made leading to an opening. He led her to it and they paused, remaining in the shadows as she looked out to see a winding path around the cliff, down onto a what appeared to be a stone bridge leading to the dark and terrible fortress on the other side. The only catch was there didn't appear to be a door there. A walkway with a high wall encircled the base of the fortress.

The fortress itself looked as though it had been carved from the mountaintop. It was difficult to make out where the fortress stopped and the mountain started. There were numerous windows up and down it and all of them were lit with a pale-yellow glow as if the inhabitants never slept. The one turret reached high into the night sky. If there were archers on the first mountain pass, she was certain there were others waiting for them along the walls of the fortress.

"I don't believe it," she whispered.

"We wind our way down the cliff and to that bridge, then follow the walkway until we find a way in," he said.

"What about guards?" she asked. "Won't there be some guarding along the walls?"

"Possibly," he said. "That's why you're going to stay here while I find out."

"You're going to leave me here?" Her heart soared into her throat.

"You'll be safe here and I'll be right back." He started to go, but she grabbed him by the arm.

"What if you don't? What do I do?" she asked.

He gave her a half grin, the corner of his mouth lifting. Then he brushed the back of his gloved hand over her cheek, the cold leather leaving a trail. "Don't worry. I *will* return."

"But what if you don't?" she demanded, trying to ignore the worry gnawing at her.

"Then you'll go back the way we came and find Gustav."

The thought of descending that steep staircase all alone made her gut clench into a tight knot. She gripped his arm tighter, pulling him a little closer, their noses nearly touching.

"You better come back for me."

With his face so close to hers, she saw his features soften despite the shadows. "I'll come for you. I promise."

Then he sealed his promise with a kiss. It surprised her so much she wasn't sure how to react. Despite the cold, his mouth was warm and wonderful against hers. His lips soft and gentle and sweet. A wild swirl of emotions whirled through her.

When he pulled away, he whispered. "Stay right here."

And then he was gone into the night.

CHAPTER 19

Nicholas headed down the path, the steep decline making it hard on his legs. He tried to keep his steps quiet so as not to alert any guards, but there didn't appear to be any on the back of the fortress. And why would there be? Most invaders would come from the front of the fortress which faced the south.

At the edge of the bridge, he paused to take in a deep breath. He peered into the darkness but saw nothing and no one and hoped that was a good sign. As he stepped out onto the bridge, he stole a glance upward where he left Ella. She was well concealed there.

Good. He didn't want her to get captured.

He scurried across the bridge heading for the walkway but all the time thinking of kissing Ella. He should not have kissed her, but she was hard to resist with the worry in her eyes.

On the ship, when they were crossing, she had looked so sad when she spoke about her stepmother and stepsisters. As if going home really wasn't an option. It sent a pang of concern through him. How could he send her back knowing she would be unhappy?

He would think about that later as he focused on crossing the bridge. He made it to the other side in record time, his breath see-sawing in and out and his lungs burning from the exertion in the frigid night air. He slipped through the opening in the wall, then pressed his back against it, glancing left and right.

Torches lined the wall every few feet, leaving puddles of light. Though he hadn't shared it with Ella, his idea was to find a couple of guards he could knock out and steal their overcoats, thereby allowing them to slip inside the fortress unnoticed. So far, no one had presented themselves as a potential victim.

He headed down the length of the wall to the left. In the distance, the walkway curved around the fortress and there were no doors visible. He hurried down he wall, his footsteps light as he approached the first torch. Ahead, a guard rounded the corner.

He pressed his back against the wall, remaining in the shadows and hoping he remained unnoticed. As the guard neared, he sized him up, hoping he was at least as tall as he was. The man wore a helm that concealed most of his face, full plate armor, a sword swinging by this side, and an overcoat with the sigil of the dark queen—a crow in flight.

Nicholas reached into the pocket of his cloak, pulling out a small corked vial. He had stashed it there before they left the castle, hoping it would come in handy. He thumbed the cork off as the guard neared and when he passed, Nicholas tossed the contents on the man.

A shimmering cloud landed on him, making him halt. He paused long enough to turn around and see Nicholas there in the shadows. As he reached for his sword, his eyes rolled back and he collapsed, landing with a muffled thud. He stuck the empty vial back in his pocket.

The sleeping powder would only work for a certain amount of time, so he had to hurry. He bent down and stripped the cloak off the guard, then wrapped it around his shoulders. It took some doing, but he managed to move the man's lifeless body to a sitting position up against the wall. Anyone passing by would assume he was sleeping on the job or passed out drunk.

Now, he had to find a suitable disguise for Ella.

Or did he?

Perhaps he could talk Ella into pretending to be his prisoner as he led her through the fortress to find Ingrid. None of the other guards would question him. And if they did, he'd tell them he was leading her to the queen.

"Hello, dear."

His mother's voice startled him out of his contemplation and he whirled to face her. She looked like the picture of Christmas standing there in her red gown trimmed in white fur with matching cloak. The hood was up, framing her face and hiding her shimmering silver hair as her bright blue eyes fixed him in disapproval.

"Mother? What are you doing here?"

"I think the more important question is what are *you* doing here?" She propped her gloved hands on her waist as she looked him over with a critical eye. "And why are you wearing *that*?"

He took her by the arm and led her away from the sleeping guard but she craned her neck to look back at him.

"What have you done?" she asked.

"Don't worry. He's not dead. Just sleeping."

"You used the sleeping powder on him?" she asked.

He nodded as they came to a halt near the exit leading back to the bridge.

"Malvina kidnapped one of the girls from the village," he said. "We're here to rescue her."

"We?" She looked around as though looking for someone else.

"Me and Ella."

"You brought Ella here?" She peered at him in astonished shock. She dropped her voice to a rough whisper. "Does she still have the slippers?"

"Yes."

"Nicholas!" This time she didn't bother to keep her voice down. "After all the trouble I went through keeping them out of Malvina's hands and you bring them right to her."

"Well, Mother, what can I say. She wouldn't leave them behind at the castle." A hint of guilt laced his words as he ran his hand through his hair, unable to meet her gaze.

"You took her to the castle?" Her voice trembled with disbelief as she clutched her chest as if trying to steady herself. The color drained from her cheeks, leaving behind a pale complexion that accentuated her distress.

"I had to."

She paced a small length of the walkway, worrying her hands. "Now she'll know who we are."

"She doesn't," he said, trying to reassure her. "Well, she knows I'm a prince."

"A prince?" She cut him a glance over her shoulder, then turned to face him. "Are you going to tell her the truth?"

"I don't know. Mother, what are you doing here?"

"When I discovered you were here, I thought you might need some help," she said. "Now, I know you do."

His eyes narrowed to slits. "Are you following me?"

"No!" she said, though there was a hint of a lie in her voice. "It's just that, well, Ella is extraordinary."

He folded his arms over the guard's thick cloak. "And?"

"And nothing," she fired back. "She's special. That's all."

"You've arranged this whole thing, haven't you? From meeting her at the ball to sending her here."

"I never intended for you to bring her into Malvina's lair," she said, her tone sharp. "Nor did I send her here on purpose. That was purely accidental."

He heaved a sigh, his breath pluming in front of him. There was no arguing with her. Once she got something in her head, she was determined to see it through no matter the cost.

"If you want to help, then find out where Malvina is holding Ingrid so we can get her and get out as quickly as possible," he said. "In the meantime, I'm going to go back for Ella."

"I'll see what I can find out. But Nicholas..." She paused, grasping him by the hand and giving it a squeeze. "Don't let Ella bring the slippers into the fortress."

"Why?"

"Because Malvina will sense their magic. In fact, she may already sense them being so close as it is."

"Perhaps you better tell me why she wants them so badly," he said.

"They're linked to the wearer's emotions," Noella said. "If Malvina gets them, she will use them to manipulate and deceive others into getting what she wants."

"And what is that?"

"The throne," she said matter-of-factly.

She didn't have to explain. Nicholas understood she meant Malvina wanted *her* throne. She wanted to crush the Spirit of Christmas once and for all, thereby destroying Rovenheim altogether. He also understood that letting Ella bring them into the fortress would be a mistake, but then, Ella wasn't going to part with them either.

"I understand," he said at last.

"I'll see what I can find out for you." Noella stood on tiptoe and kissed his cheek. "Be careful."

He gave her a nod. "You, too."

Then she was gone as quickly as she had appeared.

Nicholas crossed the bridge and made his way up the path carved into the side of the cliff and returned to Ella's hiding place. When she heard his footsteps, she poked her head out. Relief washed over her face when she saw him.

"Told you I'd be back," he said. "And I have a plan."

"Good. What is it?"

"I don't think you'll like it," he said.

She tipped her head to one side as she looked him over. "I think I can guess. You're dressed as a palace guard, so am I to assume I'll pretend to be your prisoner as we enter the fortress?"

He nodded. "Something like that."

She pressed her lips together in a thin line, clearly not happy about the situation.

"There's something else," he said, thinking about what his mother said. "You should leave the slippers here."

"Here? In this cave?"

"They'll be safe until we can return for them."

But she was already shaking her head before he finished. "No. My fairy godmother entrusted me with them. I'm keeping them with me."

His chest tightened as apprehension rolled through him at the thought of bringing the slippers into the fortress. He, of course, knew what her answer would be, but he thought it might be worth a try anyway. Finally, he nodded.

"If you insist."

"I do," she said.

He took her by the hand. "Are you ready?"

She sucked in a breath, expelled it. "As I'll ever be."

Together, they descended, crossed the bridge and headed for the fortress. They slipped inside the wall and he turned left. They passed the sleeping guard. Ella gave him a curious glance but said nothing as they moved on down the wall, heading for the curve in the walkway. He hoped they would find a way in once they made the corner.

They turned the corner, but it was merely another walkway with torches every few feet, making the stones shimmer in pools of light. But up ahead, he was certain he saw an oversized door with iron hinges leading inside.

"Look." She kept her voice soft as she pointed to it.

"I see it," he said with a nod. "That's our way in."

As they approached the door, it swung open. Yellow light spilled out onto the walkway and suddenly there were numerous guards charging out with swords drawn. Nicholas halted. Ella moved closer to him, her hand still in his as he gave it a squeeze of reassurance. But they both knew they were caught.

The guards surrounded them in a semi-circle. Only one stood before them.

The figure of a shadow elongated on the wall just inside the doorway and then she was there, moving out from the fortress onto the walkway, her black gown trailing after her as she approached the two of them. Nicholas's heart clawed its way to his throat as he made eye contact with the Queen of Darkness and Shadow.

She paused in front of him, looking him over first and then Ella with her dark, glittering eyes. She had high cheekbones, blood red lips, a pointed chin, and a thin nose.

"Well, well," she said. "It appears I've caught myself a prince. How fortunate for me. How *unfortunate* for you. Disarm him."

The lead guard stepped forward with his sword pointed at his chest. "Drop your sword."

He hesitated only a moment before he unbuckled it from his waist and let it fall to the ground. Another guard stepped forward to retrieve it.

Malvina moved to stand in front of Ella. She took her chin in her hand, turning her face from side to side.

"And who is this beauty?" Malvina asked. She cut Nicholas a sharp glance.

He refused to answer.

Malvina released Ella and stepped back. "Search her."

The guard to the queen's left stepped toward Ella, but Nicholas shoved her behind him and blocked his path.

"You stay away from her," he said.

Malvina emitted a cackle. "My dear prince, there is nothing you can do to stop him." Then she snapped her fingers.

Two guards stepped forward and took him by the arms, dragging him away from Ella. She stood tall, her hands in fists at her sides and her chin lifted in defiance. She was trying to be brave and he loved that about her. The guard moved forward again and reached for her cloak. He ripped it off her, revealing the velvet bag on her shoulder.

"Why, what's this?" Malvina stepped toward Ella, holding her hand up for the bag. "Hand it over."

Ella cut him a questioning glance. There was no way to defy the queen. He gave her a nod of defeat. Ella slipped it off her shoulder and handed it to Malvina, her shoulders slumping.

The queen pulled open the bag and peered inside, then snapped her head up at Ella. Her eyes were full of menace.

"You. You were the one who had them all along. You were hiding in the village when I destroyed their precious star. Isn't that true?"

"What if it is?" Ella said, her voice strong and sure.

Nicholas stifled the smile of pride that wanted to erupt when the queen's face turned dark and dangerous at Ella's response.

"It matters not. All that does is that I have the slippers at last. Take them to the dungeon!"

Her cackle was the last thing he heard as the guards led them away.

Chapter 20

Now that she had the slippers, Malvina left Ella and Nicholas in the custody of the guards. Ella replayed giving the queen the slippers over and over in her mind trying to decide what she could have done differently to keep them in her possession.

All this time, she had protected them, kept them with her, and made sure they were safe. Now, they were in the hands of the enemy. Perhaps she should have left them in the cave like Nicholas suggested.

Her stomach clenched with the horrifying thought of what Malvina could do with them. She recalled Alice's word, specifically that they were connected to the emotions of the wearer. What terrible things would Malvina do when she put them on and poured her hatred and her malice into them? Destroy the village? Or—worse—the kingdom?

She cut a glance at Nicholas. He must have sensed her looking at him because he gave her a small, apologetic smile.

"I'm sorry," she whispered.

"Don't be," he said. "It was my idea to come here."

She opened her mouth to protest when one of the guards snapped, "No talking."

They fell silent as they made their way down a spiral stone staircase that led down, down, down into the bowels of the fortress. The deeper they went, the colder the air turned around them. Torches lined the walls, giving off a sinister glow in the dark recesses of Malvina's dungeon.

At a gate, the lead guard paused to unlock it from a key from a ring on his belt. The key clinked in the lock, then he shoved it open. The hinges groaned as it swung open to reveal more darkness. Here the air was stale and dank.

The lead guard pulled a torch off the wall by the gate. They followed and, as they entered, Ella noticed a line of cells with iron bars on the right and the left. It was too dark to see if anyone was in those cells as they passed, but she heard the shuffle of feet in one. In another, she saw two dirty hands clutching the bars as they passed. Only the faint outline of a youthful face was visible.

Her heart lurched. How many prisoners did Malvina have down here?

The lead guard paused at one cell, unlocked it and opened the door. Nicholas was shoved inside that one. The door slammed shut. Across from that cell, he unlocked another one. The guard behind her pushed her inside. The door slammed shut with a resounding bang.

The guards said nothing as they left them there to rot in the darkness. Silence descended. Far down the corridor, the other gate slammed closed, sealing their fate.

Ella took a look at her new home. A pile of straw was in one corner. A dirty chamber pot in another, as though it had never been removed from the previous occupant. Her stomach lurched as bile rose to her throat. She turned away, moving closer to the bars where there was a patch of light from a nearby torch.

She peered out of the bars, trying to see Nicholas, but he was deep in the shadows of his cell. She heard a scraping noise.

"Nicholas?"

"I'm going to find a way out of here," he said, his disembodied voice coming from the dark.

More scraping noises.

"What are you doing?" she asked.

"They may have taken my sword, but I still have my dagger."

"You do?" She hadn't seen that on him.

"Hidden in my cloak." *Scrape. Scape. Scape.*

She caught a glimpse of him as he passed in front of the cell door, then more scraping noises.

"This mortar is weak," he said, his voice strained with exertion.

"Even if you managed to get out, how are we going to get past the locked gate?" she asked.

He stopped scraping and silence descended, then he said, "I'll worry about that after we get out of here."

He sounded so confident it was hard not to believe him. Ella peered out of her cell bars, straining her eyes to see movement across from her. She saw a flash of his hand every now and then as the scraping continued.

Footsteps echoed in the stone hallway. But not the thump of boots. No, this was at a much faster clip as the shoes struck the stone with every step. The woman came into view then wearing a thick hooded cloak concealing her face. She flung off her hood revealing shining silvery hair piled high on her head and propped her fists on her hips.

"Fairy godmother?" Ella breathed. She was truly shocked to see her fairy godmother here.

The scraping came to an abrupt halt. Nicholas's face appeared between two of the bars as he looked out.

"What are you doing here?" he asked, not bothering to hide his surprise. "And how did you get in here?"

She ignored his first question. "I see I can't leave you two unsupervised." She huffed out a sigh. "The girl from the village is two cells down." She nodded backward.

"Gee, thanks. Did you come to help us or merely give us that information?"

"Don't be cheeky," she snapped. "I told you not to come here. Especially with the..." She paused, glancing around, and then whispered, "...slippers." As she said it, she looked at Ella.

Guilt swarmed through Ella as the heat rose to her cheeks. "I-I'm sorry. It's my fault. I should have left them hidden in the cave, but I was worried—"

"Pish posh, dear. No need to explain. I know why you did it."

"You do?"

She nodded. "Of course, I do. You were trying to protect them and keep them safe. However..." She cut Nicholas a glance. "I specifically said *not* to bring them into the fortress."

"You did," he agreed with a nod. "Now that we've established what a terrible idea it was, are you going to help us or not?"

Something about the way he spoke to Noella made it seem he was familiar with her. Ella tipped her head to the side, trying to understand their dynamics.

"I can get you out and past the gate but that's all. I shouldn't even be here."

She stepped up to his cell door and pulled out a magic wand seemingly out of the air. She pointed it at the key hole. Sparks flew as she used it to melt the lock. The cell door came open with ease. Nicholas stepped out, sheathing his dagger. Then she turned to Ella's cell and did the same. When the door was open, she stepped out.

"The girl is just down here." Noella motioned to the other cell.

"What about the others here?" Ella asked.

Noella paused, turning back to her with question in her eyes. "Others?"

"There are more prisoners here," Ella said.

"Ella, we don't know why they're here or who they are," Nicholas said. "They could be dangerous."

"And they could be innocent like Ingrid," she countered.

"Who's Ingrid?" Noella asked.

"The girl from the village," Nicholas said.

"Eh! Are ye goin' to let me out, too?" someone called from one of the cells.

"No!" Noella shouted, then to Ella, "Perhaps if we had more time, dear, we could do that. For now, we must make haste."

Without waiting for an answer, Noella hurried down to the cell with the girl in it. She used her wand to open the cell door and then waited. There was no movement.

"You're safe now, dearest. We're going to take you home." She waved for the girl to come out of the cell.

When there was still no movement, Noella huffed. Her wand disappeared back into the air, then she put her hands on her hips once more.

"We must go, little one."

Still nothing.

"Let me try," Ella said as she stepped around Noella into the doorway of the cell.

She looked into the cell to see a scared young girl huddled against the far wall. Her clothes were torn and dirty. The cell smelled awful. Her face was dirty, her eyes were round with fear. She had two long braids, one over each shoulder.

"Hi," Ella said, her voice soft. "You're Ingrid, right?"

The girl considered whether or not to answer, then finally nodded.

"I'm Ella," she said. "I know your grandmother, Agnes. She helped me when I was lost." Ella took a tentative step inside the cell.

Some of the tension in Ingrid's body dissipated.

"She told me all about you," Ella continued.

"She...did?" A soft mewl from the girl.

Ella nodded. "Yes. You're thirteen. And you have a sister. And your father is the apothecary in the village."

Ingrid straightened a little as she nodded again.

"My friends and I have come to take you home," Ella said. "This is Nicholas." She waved for him to come into the cell.

He stepped to Ella's side and gave a small wave. "Hello."

"And this is Noella." Ella stepped a little closer and said in a rough pretend-whisper, "She's my fairy godmother."

That got her attention. "Your fairy godmother?"

Behind her, Noella huffed. Nicholas shushed her with a slash of his hand.

Ella held her hand out to Ingrid. "Yes, and she's going to help us get out of here. And then we'll take you home."

"You promise?"

"Promise."

Ingrid reached for her hand, sliding it into Ella's. The girl's hand was cold as she took it and a pang of concern went through her. Ingrid had no cloak but at least she still had on her wool dress and boots. Ella pulled her to her, wrapping a protective arm around her shoulders.

"Let's go," Noella said.

She charged down the corridor heading for the gate. Seconds later, she had it open, too. She pulled it open and stepped aside. Ella and Ingrid were first followed by Nicholas who turned to face Noella.

"Are you coming?" he asked, concern lining his face.

"I can't. You know why. The two of you will be fine. Follow the staircase up. At the top, turn left and then take that hallway back to the door. That will lead you outside to the walkway. Then you know the rest of the way," she said.

"But the slippers—" Ella began.

Noella shook her head. "Those are lost to us, now, dear. She has them. She won't give them up. Now go." She shooed them down the hallway.

Nicholas stepped closer, dropping his voice and said something to her Ella was unable to hear. Noella gave him a smile, then kissed his cheek.

"I'll be fine," she said, her eyes sparkling with something Ella couldn't read.

Nicholas turned back to Ella and Ingrid. "Let's go then."

They started down the corridor, back the way they came not long ago. Ella stole a glance over her shoulder, but Noella was gone. The only thing that remained was a puff of glitter in the air, as if she had disappeared into it.

Nicholas took the lead. Ella kept her arm around Ingrid as they hurried behind him, but the girl shivered against her.

"Just a moment," she said, coming to a halt.

Nicholas paused, turning to chastise her to hurry when he realized what she was doing. Ella pulled off her gloves and handed them to the girl. Relief went over Ingrid's face as she pulled on the gloves.

"And this," he said, moving toward them.

He pulled off his cloak and wrapped it around the girl, closing the clasp at her throat. It was much too long for her and dragged the ground but it would keep her warm.

"There now. Better?" he asked.

Ingrid nodded.

"Thank you," Ella said.

"Now come. We have to hurry," he said.

They hurried to the stone staircase and started to ascend. It wound up, up, up to the top, leaving them all breathless. Ella's legs burned and she thought she couldn't take one more step as they reached the top.

Nicholas paused long enough to catch his breath. She took several deep breaths trying to slow her erratic heart. Ingrid clung to her waist, her breath see-sawing in and out. He gave Ella a questioning glance. She nodded to keep going.

He started down the hallway, pulling his dagger from the sheath at his waist. She and Ingrid followed. She kept the girl close to her.

As they rounded a corner, a deep rumbling started somewhere in the fortress. Nicholas came to an abrupt halt. Ella almost ran into the back of him. The rumble sounded again.

"That can't be good," he said.

"What is it?" Ella whispered. Her voice shook with the nerves that suddenly erupted.

"Not sure but we should keep going."

He started again. They took several steps when the rumbling happened again.

Malvina appeared at the end of the corridor in a puff of purple smoke. In her hands, she carried the glass slippers as she stormed toward them.

"Not good at all," Nicholas muttered.

He held his dagger at the ready. She and Ingrid remained behind him, waiting and watching as the dark queen approached. Fury was etched on her face.

"You..." Her narrowed, terrible eyes fixed on Ella, then cut to Nicholas and the girl. "How did you get out of your cell?"

"I don't think that matters now," Nicholas said.

She cut a glance to his dagger. "Do you think that little weapon of yours will stop me?" She shook her head. "The girl and I have unfinished business."

"You can't have her," Ella said, clutching Ingrid close to her.

"Oh, dear sweet child. I meant *you*," she said, fixing her eyes on Ella. "You're going to tell me how to use these slippers."

"Never," Ella said.

"And you'll have to go through me to get to her," Nicholas added.

Malvina's eyes narrowed. "So be it."

Clutching the slippers in one hand, she waved her other one. Nicholas flew to the side and crashed against the stone wall. He slipped down it, landing on the ground unconscious with a thud.

"Nicholas!" Ella gasped.

"The slippers, girl," she said as she approached. "Tell me how to use them."

"I-I don't know," she said.

"Do not lie to me."

"I'm not." Ella backed away a step at a time as Ingrid scurried to Nicholas's side. "They were a gift."

Malvina halted her advance. "A gift, you say?" Contemplation went over her face before she then smiled a dark and terrible smile. "How nice."

The dark queen waved her hand in an elaborate gesture sending purple smoke curling toward Ella. She took a step back, intending to run back to the staircase, but the cloud overcame her. A sudden dizziness swept over her as she stumbled to the side. Her vision blurred. The last thing she saw was Malvina advancing on her once again with that terrible smile. And then there was nothing at all.

CHAPTER 21

E lla awoke with a raging headache throbbing in her left
temple. Her arms were strained behind her, the muscles
at her shoulders burning with an intensity she had never experienced. It took several moments for her to pry her eyes open.
She blinked, looking on unfamiliar surroundings.

She was tied to a chair, her arms behind her and her wrists
bound. She tugged on the rope but found it held fast and
chafed her skin. She was in some sort of chamber with an
oversized fireplace on one end, a large bed on another. Balcony
doors were open, letting in the bitter north wind, the curtains
fluttering in the breeze.

On the balcony, Malvina stood with her back to her. Her
hands were on the railing as she peered out at the mountains
beyond. It was dawn as far as Ella could tell. The sky was lit in
a pale indigo tinged with pink.

A guard stood at the entrance of the chamber. He stood with
his hands clasped in front of him, wearing full armor. His face
was concealed behind a helm.

A whimper next to her caught Ella's attention. She turned her head to see Nicholas and Ingrid tied together to chairs, back-to-back, and gaged. Their wrists were also bound. Their ankles tied to the chair legs. His head hung down, his chin on his chest, as though he were still unconscious. Ingrid watched her with frightened eyes. She glanced from Ella's face, down and back up again.

She was trying to tell her something.

Then she understood. Her boots and thick stockings were gone. One foot was bare. On the other, she wore one of the glass slippers. She held up her foot to examine it. The shoe seemed unharmed.

Malvina turned from the balcony, the wind whipping through her long, black hair as she made her way back inside. She paused in the doorway, her dark eyes falling on Ella.

"Awake, I see. Good."

The train of her black gown slithered over the stones as she entered the room, leaving the doors open. The cold wind whipped through the room, sending a violent chill through Ella. Malvina paused at the mantle where she picked up the other shoe. She held it between her hands as she approached. Light sparkled through the shoe, giving it an iridescent glow.

"You're going to tell me how to use this." She waved the second slipper at Ella.

Ella lifted her chin in defiance. "I already told you I don't know how it works."

She stared at her a long, hard moment. Then she whirled around. She grabbed another nearby chair and pulled it over in front of Ella. She positioned herself on the edge, still holding the shoe in her hands.

"Let me show you something."

She slipped off her black shoe, crossing her legs to reach her foot. Then she tried to put on the glass slipper.

It wouldn't fit. Only her toes and the ball of her foot were able to slide inside. The rest of her foot was too big. She held it up for Ella to see, then cast an accusatory glance at Ella's foot wearing the other one.

"Care to explain that?" the dark queen asked.

Ella peered down at her foot, then at Malvina's as her heartbeat quickened. The shoe, it seemed, did not want to fit Malvina's foot. Perhaps the magical properties of it had something to do with that. Alice's words came tumbling back to her.

It is said they can only be worn by the person they're meant for.

Ella's mouth went dry. She swallowed hard as the realization came. The slippers, it seemed, were meant for her.

The slippers led her to her true love. *Nicholas.* It took all her willpower not to cut him a glance.

The slippers were connected to the emotions of the wearer. *Her* emotions. Right now, her emotions were erratic as they pounded through her. From fear to uncertainty to a glimmer of hope she and her friends had a chance to get out of Malvina's fortress alive.

"Well?" Malvina prompted when she didn't answer.

"Legend says they can only be worn by the person they're meant for," Ella said, her voice strong and sure.

"Legend!" she scoffed. She pulled off the shoe and shoved back from the chair and started to pace, the slipper clutched in her hand. "Do you expect me to believe that fairy tale?"

Despite her quivering gut, Ella remained strong. "Why does the slipper not fit you then if it's not true?"

She halted, spinning to face her with narrowed eyes. "Who are you? And how did you get these slippers?" She shook the shoe at her.

"I told you. Someone gifted them to me."

"Ha! And that someone was Noella Fairchild, that meddlesome fairy, I'll wager."

Heat swarmed up Ella's neck as she clenched her jaw. Malvina flung herself around and headed for a tapestry on a nearby wall. She pulled it back to reveal the massive mirror in an ornate gold frame. Fog floated through the mirror and then a face with nothing but round holes for eyes, nose, and a mouth appeared.

"Dark Mirror, tell me what I seek. Who gifted the girl the slippers?"

"Noella Fairchild, my dark and beautiful queen," the mirror said.

Malvina turned back to Ella. "The mirror never lies." She took slow, methodical steps toward her. "But you do. Do you know what I do to those who lie to me?"

Ella remained silent. Her stomach clenched.

The queen chuckled, a sound deep in her throat. "I kill them. But you...you're special, aren't you?" She stood in front of Ella now and bent down, placing a long, slender finger under her chin and tipped her face upward so she stared right into those dark, depthless, terrifying eyes. "Noella chose you. What, then, will she do to make sure no harm comes to you, hm?"

"Enough, Malvina," Nicholas snapped in a raspy voice. "Get away from her."

Ella snapped her head in his direction. Somehow, he had managed to remove the gag to under his chin. Their eyes met. His were full of apology, as though he blamed himself for their capture.

Malvina straightened and pinned him with her best glare.

"Quite resourceful, aren't you? But you are in no position to make demands, prince." She tapped the ball of the shoe against the palm of her hand as she peered down at Ella. "Let's put this other slipper on you, shall we?"

She bent and slipped the shoe on her foot. It was a perfect fit.

The moment the slipper was on her other foot, Ella felt a strong surge of what she assumed was magic shooting through her. It was as if the magic only worked when she had on both shoes.

Malvina pressed her fingertips together, tapping her forefingers in a rhythmic way as she considered Ella. She glanced from the slippers to her face and back again.

"Now, here's what we're going to do. You're going to use those slippers to get what I want."

"And what is that?" Ella asked.

"Why, Rovenheim's throne, of course," she replied.

"No," Nicholas said. "You will *never* get that."

"Silence!" she snapped at him.

"I will not help you," Ella said, defiant.

She dropped her hands to her side, a sort of sadness coming over her features. "Pity."

Without warning, Malvina flung her hands toward Ella. A blast of dark magic hit her square in the chest. She cried out as her head fell backward with the burning sensation clawing through her.

"That was a warning," Malvina said.

Tears stung Ella's eyes. Tears of anger and fear and pain. The slippers on her feet responded to that, sending a pulse into the room that looked like shimmering light. Malvina sucked in a sharp breath when it hit her. She pressed a hand against her gut. She faced Ella with suspicion creasing her face.

"Ah...so you *do* know how to use them."

Ella blinked the tears from her vision as they fell down her cheeks. "I...will not...help you," she repeated. The pain of speaking was nearly unbearable.

"Then perhaps you need a different sort of motivation."

She waved her hands into a tight circle and conjured a table topped with an oversized hourglass. Inside, black sand rested at the bottom. Malvina grasped it, holding it, and pinpointing Ella with her evil glare. Then she turned it over to allow the sand to run from the top to the bottom.

"You have until the sand runs out to give me what I want."

With a wave of her hand, she disappeared in a puff of purple haze.

Ella sniffed, trying to keep the tears at bay. A weight pressed against her chest with dread.

Another shimmering wave emanated from her, filling the room with sparkling air that reminded her of dust motes dancing in the sunlight.

"Ella?" Her name was a tentative question on his lips. "I know you're scared and upset. I can sense it from here."

Was that from the shoes? She glanced down at them. They shimmered with the same sort of wavy light dancing in the room. She took a deep breath. Crying was going to get her nowhere. She needed to pull herself together and figure out a plan. She worked at the knots behind her back, the ropes chafing her skin.

"I'm sorry, Ella," he said.

"For what?" She glanced at him, trying to shove back her guilt. "It's my fault. All of this. If I just removed the slippers before the last stroke of midnight like I was supposed to, none of this would be happening."

"If you removed the slippers before the last stroke of midnight, I'd have never seen you again."

Her heart lurched and her pulse raced at his words. He was right. She'd never be here in Rovenheim and he would be lost to her. Instead, she'd be stuck back at home with her terrible stepmother and stepsisters, slaving every day away as though she was nothing. At least here, she was made to feel as if she was something. Even if it was the dark queen's prisoner.

She continued to work the rope around her wrists. Her hands were slick. She assumed that was due to either blood or sweat or both. It didn't matter. She had to find a way to get out of those bonds so she could help Nicholas and Ingrid before the sands ran out.

If only the slippers could help her. She closed her eyes, thinking positive thoughts, trying to will the knots to come undone.

An idea struck her. She eyed the guard standing at the entrance of the chamber.

She scooted her chair, scraping it along the stone floor to face the guard. She hooked one foot around a leg of the chair and pushed. Her muscles quivered with the exertion, but she managed to turn it around to face him.

She planted her feet together in front of her, her toes pointing at the guard.

Think, Ella, think.

If the slippers were truly connected to her emotions, then perhaps she could use it to her advantage. What sort of emotion, though, would coerce the guard to free her?

"Hello, there," she said and gave him her best smile.

If he looked at her, she was unable to see. He was several feet away and the helm hid his expression from her.

"Could you help me?" she asked.

The guard remained motionless.

She stole a glance to the hourglass to see about half the sand was gone from the top. Her heartbeat quickened. She had to get this guard to cooperate with her before the sand ran out and Malvina returned.

"My hands are tied, you see," she continued, using her sweetest voice. "Do you suppose you could untie me?"

There was a flicker of movement as he flinched. She wasn't sure, but she thought his head turned to her. He took a tentative step forward.

"I know your hands are tied," he said, his voice gruff.

"Yes, well, if you untie me..." She paused, trying to think of some way to get him to cooperate. "I'll reward you."

He tipped his head to one side. "Reward me how?"

She flashed a bright smile. "I can't tell you that until you untie me." She scooted her feet forward. "Please?"

A wave of magic pulsed from the toes of the slippers. She watched the shimmering glow as it floated through the air and then settled around him. He was spurred into action.

"Of course, my lady."

He moved behind her and tugged on the ropes. Moments later, she was free from the chair.

"There you are, my lady. Now, for my reward...?" He gave her a wicked grin and started to reach for her.

Ella's heart was in her throat. Her hands shook as she spun and grasped the chair in both hands, picking it up. It was heavier than she expected and for a moment she faltered. She recovered quickly, swinging the heavy wooden chair and connected it with the side of his head. He stumbled backward, yanking off his helm. He spun, his face red with anger.

Sucking in a sharp breath, she swung the chair again. It smacked into him across his shoulder and the side of his head. He went down in a heap, landing on the floor with a muffled thump.

"Ella!" Nicholas gasped.

Ignoring him, she hurried over to first Ingrid. She pulled off the girl's gag, then started working on her ropes.

"They're too tight."

"Get my dagger," he said.

"They didn't take it?"

"Worst guards ever," he replied with a little laugh.

She grabbed the dagger out of his sheath and sawed through his bonds. It took precious long minutes but she finally managed to free him. He took the dagger from her and went to free Ingrid.

"Your wrists, Ella," he said as he removed the girl's ropes.

She glanced down to see her wrists were angry, raw, and bleeding. "I'll be fine. Where are my boots?"

"I'll get you more boots. Whatever you do, *do not* take those slippers off," he said. "Now, let's get out of here."

She started to protest but then decided he had a point. Keeping the slippers on would keep them out of Malvina's hands. She'd worry about walking back to the ship in them later. As they hurried out of the chamber, she stole a backward glance at the hourglass as the last few grains of sand emptied.

Malvina appeared in her cloud of purple smoke. Fury immediately crossed her face. She emitted a howl of frustration and charged after them.

Ella stumbled in the slippers. Nicholas wrapped a hand around her upper arm to help her maintain her balance. The delay caused them precious seconds as Malvina charged up behind them. She sent a beam of magic, punching Nicholas in the back. He stumbled forward, falling and taking Ella with him. Ingrid jumped out of the way, pressing her back against the wall.

Malvina stood over them, her face lined with anger.

"I see how determined you are to escape me," she said. "But you will not leave this place alive." Her eyes, filled with a burning rage, bored into Nicholas like fiery daggers. "Unless, prince..."

He pulled himself back up to his feet, helping Ella do the same.

"Unless what?" he asked.

"Unless your mother bends the knee, pledges allegiance to me, and steps down from her throne." She held her hands open at her side, as though ready to fling more deadly magic at him.

"She will *never* do that," Nicholas said.

"So be it."

She raised her arms, purple flames dancing in her palms. Nicholas shoved Ella behind him to protect her. But she was more worried about him. She grabbed him by the hand and started tugging him backward toward the exit.

Ingrid scurried behind them, heading away from Malvina and her wrath. The dark queen released her purple flames.

As Ella watched the wave ripple toward them, something strange happened. Suddenly, a blinding white light emerged between them and the dark magic. And then, Noella appeared before them, blocking Malvina's malevolence.

"That will be quite enough, *sister*."

CHAPTER 22

ister? Noella Fairchild, her fairy godmother, was Malvina's sister?

Ella sucked in a sharp breath as she looked from Noella to Malvina. Ingrid halted her sprint and instead moved to stand next to Ella. She wrapped an arm around the girl's shoulders, pulling her close. Nicholas stood in front of them both like a shield.

Noella's silvery hair hung in loose waves down her back. Instead of her normal festive gowns, she wore trousers, boots, a thick tunic and a cloak fastened at her neck with a star pin. She held her wand in her hand, the point of it lit brightly in white light.

"Get out of my way, Noella." She held her hands ready to release more dark magic.

"I will not," she said, defiant. She lifted her chin. "Nor will the throne be relinquished to you."

Malvina growled with her frustration. "You stole those slippers from me. I want them back."

"You and I both know you have nothing but ill intentions for those slippers. And besides," she paused, gave Ella a quick glance, "they're with their rightful owner now."

"The girl is *nothing* and doesn't deserve them!"

"Oh, she's not nothing and she *does* deserve them," Noella countered.

A warmth spread through Ella's chest at her fairy godmother's words. For the first time in a long while, she was finally worthy to someone.

In Malvina's anger, she threw another ball of dark magic toward Noella. She countered it with her white magic, using her wand to turn it into nothing but harmless snowflakes. She spun back to face Nicholas, shooing him toward the exit.

"Go. Your pirate captain and Gustav are waiting for you at the gates."

Nicholas opened his mouth to ask more questions, but Noella shooed him away. She spun back around to face Malvina who was still intent on attacking.

So intent, in fact, she turned herself into a crow. She dive-bombed Ella, crashing into her back and pecking the back of her head. Ella cried out, flailing her arms to try to get Malvina away from her. Behind her, Ingrid screamed—the first sound she'd made since leaving the cell.

"Do something!" Nicholas shouted to Noella.

A flash of light and then the crow made a strangled sound and flapped higher up toward the ceiling. Nicholas caught Ella in his arms, pulling her close and holding her.

"Are you all right?" he asked.

She nodded. Sweat trickled down the side of her face and her cheeks were damp with tears. She reached up and touched the back of her head, probing the place Malvina pecked with a gentle touch.

"I'm fine," she croaked.

Noella wasn't finished with Malvina, though. She charged past them and followed as the bird flapped its way back inside the bedchamber, cawing at the top of her lungs the entire time.

"Run!" Noella ordered.

"But—" Nicholas started.

"Now!"

The door to the chamber slammed shut, sealing them both inside. Nicholas took Ella's hand and started down the corridor. Ingrid was already halfway down it, her boots thumping on the stone floor and the too-large cloak flapping behind her.

"Will she be all right?" Ella asked.

"I hope so," he replied.

Behind them, purple and white light illuminated around the door. Sounds of an altercation wafted through it. A crash and then a pounding followed by something thumping against the door. Ella hoped her fairy godmother would make it out alive.

"I've just about had enough of you," Noella said.

She clutched her wand, hesr palm sweating, as she watched the bird flap around the room. She shot a bit of magic toward her and missed.

Malvina returned to her true form, the purple smoke billowing around her in a cloud.

"And I've had enough of *you*," Malvina said. "You've taken everything from me once again."

"I'm not the one who used dark magic and got herself banished." It was a cheap shot, Noella knew, but it served the purpose.

Malvina's face pinched with fury. "I'm not the one who sucked up to father all those years. You're not so innocent yourself."

She threw a bomb of magic at her. Noella ducked behind a chair.

"I'm not the one who used the Dark Mirror." Noelle fired back with her own white magic. The punch of power hit the hourglass, destroying it.

"And I'm not the one who stole the glass slippers out from under someone else!" Malvina attacked again. The cushion on the chair exploded in a puff of stuffing.

Noella moved out from behind it, looking for another place of refuge. She spotted the tapestry on the wall and knew it hid the Dark Mirror. Destroying that would be in vengeance for Malvina destroying the Christmas Star. She tossed a bit of magic at Malvina, hitting her in the shoulder long enough to distract her, then hurried over to the tapestry. She shoved it aside.

The mirror came alive with its fogginess followed by the strange magical face.

"Yes, my queen—who are you?" it said.

"Step away from that!" Malvina shouted.

Noella cut her a glance over her shoulder and took two steps back. "As you wish."

Then she pointed her wand at the mirror and sent a bright beam of light right into its center. It shattered into a thousand pieces, leaving nothing behind but the ornate gold frame.

"NO!" Then she growled, a sound deep in her throat. "You will *pay for that*!"

"That's for the Christmas Star," Noella said, a smugness overtaking her. "And to stop you from seeing into our lives."

"Those slippers belong to *me*!" Malvina whined.

"They don't. They're with their rightful owner now. Ella earned them. Ella will keep them."

"I will *destroy* you," Malvina said.

"You can try." Noella clutched her wand at her side and despite her fear, her voice remained calm. "Your dark magic is no match for mine, for I have the Light of Christmas and carry its Spirit with me wherever I go."

"Yes, yes, yes. Spreading good will and cheer." Malvina spit on the cold stone floor. "While I rot in here in my fortress."

"A fortress of your own making," Noella countered. "Farewell, sister. Perhaps we will meet again under better circumstances."

Noella placed a bubble of protection around her as she walked toward the door. But she knew Malvina wasn't finished yet. She sensed her attack before it even happened and spun to face her, using her wand to punch her sister in the middle of the chest. Malvina flew backward, landing on the stone floor and sliding several feet before coming to a halt. Noella paused, waiting to see if she would rise again. She didn't.

She walked to her, knelt, and placed two fingers on the side of her neck. There was a faint pulse. She would live.

Noella rose to her full height, a pang of sorrow for her sister going through her. She hated that she would be here, alone, for the rest of her days, but then, Malvina brought that all upon herself. Her last act would be to place a spell over the fortress, so her sister couldn't hurt anyone again.

But now, she had to make sure Ella, Nicholas, and the young Ingrid made it out of the fortress to safety. She hurried to the door, passing by the shards of mirror and noticed they had dimmed from shimmering and bright to dull and dark. The magic inside the mirror was destroyed. She knew her sister had the mirror, knew she used it to spy on her, knew she used it to plan her way to claim the throne of Rovenheim for herself. Now, with the mirror gone, Noella would finally have peace of mind.

She stepped over the glass and into the hall, leaving her sister behind once and for all.

Chapter 23

Ella followed Nicholas down the hallway to a set of stairs. He led the way down with Ingrid in between them. At the bottom, a guard waited. Nicholas wasted no time in disarming him and taking his sword. He pulled the dagger from his waist and handed it to her.

"Here. Just in case."

She clutched the dagger in her sweaty palm, not sure how to use it but grateful for the weapon nonetheless. Ingrid clung to her side as they charged into the grand hall.

And were confronted with a swarm of guards, forcing them back to the wall. One of them, who appeared to be in charge, stepped toward Nicholas with his sword raised.

"It's back to the dungeons for you all," he said.

Ella watched as Nicholas took in the surroundings, glanced upward, then to the side. An idea ignited in his eyes. He gave them a smile.

"Are you certain about that?"

He swung his sword, not at the guard, but at a rope tied off near his head. He sliced through it cleanly. Overhead, a candelabra fell from the ceiling, trapping the rest of them. Nicholas ran around them, heading for the exit, Ella and Ingrid followed.

They were almost home free.

Until they made it into the courtyard and realized they were once again faced with more guards. None of them noticed their arrival since they were busy with whoever was on the outside of the wall—Captain Bart and Gustav, no doubt. But they were a skeleton crew. How could they hold their own against so many of Malvina's men?

"We should have gone out the way we came in," Nicholas said.

"Don't worry, dear."

Noella arrived in a puff of glittering magic. With a wave of her hand, she tossed something shimmering at the three of them. Ella coughed and sputtered. So did Ingrid. Nicholas merely closed his eyes and took it as if it was something he was used to dealing with.

"The concealment spell won't last long," she said, urgency in her voice.

"What about you?" Nicholas turned to her, gripping her by the arm.

"I have one more task to accomplish."

Nicholas started to protest when she poofed away again.

"Let's go," he said with a wave.

Ella and Ingrid exchanged a glance as they took off after Nicholas. He wove his way around the men who seemed not to notice them at all. With her heart in her throat and the dagger clutched in her hand, they were almost to the gate.

It was difficult to traverse the rocky ground, though, in the slippers. She tripped and started to fall. She managed to release the dagger, throwing her arms out to break her fall as she crashed against the ground.

Ingrid gasped. "Ella!"

Nicholas halted and spun toward them as Ella turned round to sit. Her right ankle throbbed and her left wrist ached. She grimaced, as she tried to get to her feet, but it hurt too much. Nicholas was at her side in an instant. He wrapped a hand around her upper arm and helped her to her feet. She sucked in a sharp breath through her teeth when she tried to put weight on her right foot.

"You're hurt," he said.

Ingrid bounced from one foot to the other in front of her, her youthful face creased with worry.

"I twisted my ankle," she said. "It hurts to put weight on it."

The gate was too far away for her to hobble to it, especially in the slippers.

"I don't think I can make it," she added.

"You have to make it," Ingrid said as tears pooled in her eyes.

"I'm not leaving you here." Nicholas tossed the sword to the ground. He removed the dagger sheath from around his waist. "Ingrid, grab that dagger. We may need it yet."

She bent to pick up the dagger Ella discarded when she fell. He handed her the sheath. She stuck it inside as though she were a natural at such things, then tied it around her waist. Nicholas wasted no more time as he scooped her up into his arms, holding her close to his chest. Ingrid's face broke into a bright smile.

"You're going to carry her?" she asked.

Nicholas met Ella's gaze and her pulse throbbed wildly. "I am. Lead the way, Miss Ingrid."

The girl took off at a sprint. Ella wrapped her arms around his neck and held on as he started for the gate. Not at a run like Ingrid, but at a brisk pace that jostled her against him.

She didn't mind.

His body was warm and solid next to hers.

"When we get back..." he panted, "I'll have my healer look you over."

She opened her mouth to protest.

"I'll not take no for an answer." He gave her a wry smile.

Ingrid was out the gate and spun to face them, waving them on with desperation to hurry. Finally, Nicholas and Ella made it out of the walls of Malvina's fortress. He paused to catch his breath, lowering her slowly to the ground. He kept an arm wrapped around her waist to steady her and keep the weight off her injured foot.

Ahead, she saw Captain Bart, Gustav, and a few of the sailors crouched behind a line of trees firing off arrows toward the guards on the wall.

"Look!" Ingrid pointed, seeing them, too.

"Captain Bart really was here to save us," Nicholas said, as though he were surprised.

"You didn't believe Noella?"

He chuckled. "She surprises me sometimes, so I should have. She must have helped them here. Can you walk?"

"If you help me," Ella said. "I think I can manage."

"Hopefully that concealment spell is still working," Nicholas said.

Ingrid took off at a run toward the group, clearly ready to be done with Malvina's fortress and all her guards. Ella stifled a chuckle. Nicholas's arm tightened around her waist as he helped her limp toward them. Thankfully, they made it behind the tree line without anyone noticing them. The concealment spell must still be intact.

As they approached, she heard the distinct whinny of a horse.

It seemed her fairy godmother thought of everything.

Suddenly, the firing arrows stopped and everything went silent. Ella, still clutched by Nicholas, glanced back toward the fortress. The guards were no longer along the wall. As if they had merely disappeared.

Noella appeared, her long silvery hair billowing in the late morning breeze.

"Well, now. That was fun, wasn't it?" She flashed a bright smile.

"What happened to them?" Gustav asked, glancing from her to the fortress and back again.

"No need to worry about that, captain. Just know Malvina, Queen of Darkness and Shadow," she snorted at the title, "will be of no more bother to the rest of us. Now...where is my son?"

"Here, Mother." Nicholas cleared his throat.

Ella's head snapped in his direction. "Noella is your *mother*?"

"Ah, yes, of course dear." Noella blew a handful of fai ry dust their direction. It landed on all three of them, removing the concealment spell.

Ella stared at her fairy godmother and then cut a glance at Nicholas. "*She's* the queen of Rovenhcim?"

"She is." Nicholas gave her an affirmative nod.

"And you are...the crown prince?" Which was something she already knew, but she wanted to confirm that she was, in fact, standing in the arms of the prince of Rovenheim.

"Of course, he is, dear," Noella said.

She looked from Nicholas to Noella and back again. It was as if her vision cleared and she saw the family resemblance. He had his mother's eyes and the same cheeky smile.

It was all too much for Ella. The blood rushed to her head, leaving pinpricks of tiny dark spots and making her lightheaded. She did the only thing she knew to do and fainted straightaway.

CHAPTER 24

"**. . .** and then he picked her up and carried her the *whole* way to the gate!"

Ella awoke to Ingrid's excited voice and the soft rocking of the ship. She wasn't sure who she was regaling the tale of their escape from Malvina's fortress, but hearing her enthusiasm for the way Nicholas carried her to the gate made her smile.

"Well, then, I'd say he's a hero." It was Gustav who replied with a smile in his voice.

"He is. Oh, she's awake!"

The edge of her bed bounced as Ingrid perched on the side of it. Ella opened her eyes to the girl's dirty but beaming face and was unable to stop the smile that erupted.

"Hi, Ella!"

My goodness, she was a ball of energy now that she was out of the fortress and in safe hands. She had deep brown eyes in a pixie face. Despite her beaming face, she had dark circles under her eyes. Even so, one day, she was going to be a stunning beauty.

Her long hair was plaited on each side of her head. Sprigs of hair sprouted from the braids. Her face was smeared with dirt. Her hands looked as though they had a good scrubbing, but there was still dirt under her fingernails. She still wore Nicholas's cloak.

"Hi, Ingrid," Ella said with a grin.

She took in her surroundings. She was in a spacious cabin that could only belong to the captain. Gustav sat in a chair on the far side of the room, his foot propped up on a table. He had a bandage around his other leg. Noella stood off to one side, her lovely face creased with concern and then relief when Ella opened her eyes. And, then, there was Nicholas. He perched in a small chair next to her bed and smiled when their eyes met. A knee-melting smile of relief that told her everything she needed to know.

"Let me see to the patient," Nicholas said.

He gave the girl a gentle nudge. Reluctantly, she shifted down to the end of the bed. He lifted her hand, holding it. It was only then Ella realized her wrist had been bandaged. Both of them, actually. Her twisted ankle still throbbed, but it appeared to be nothing more serious. She still wore the slippers as she laid on top of the blankets in what appeared to be the captain's quarters.

"How are you feeling?" he asked, concern lining his face.

"Better, I think." When she recalled fainting in his arms, her cheeks flushed hot burning to the roots of her hair. "I-I'm sorry about—"

"Now, don't you worry your pretty head about that." Noella moved to stand behind Nicholas.

Her silvery hair was once again piled high on her head and she wore the most beautiful silver gown trimmed in white sparkling fur. Her blue eyes twinkled with mirth. Ella should have made the connection sooner, especially when she learned Nicholas was the crown prince of Rovenheim. But she hadn't.

"Glad to see you're awake." She grinned.

"Me, too," Ingrid added, still beaming.

Ella struggled to sit up. Nicholas helped her, fluffing pillows behind her back to give her some cushion. She got a good look at her surroundings and saw she was, in fact, in a spacious cabin on the ship.

"It seems Captain Bart took a liking to you," Nicholas said. "Especially after you fainted."

"This is his cabin?" she asked.

"It is." He nodded.

"I will have to properly thank him for that." She glanced down at the slippers still on her feet. "And I should return the slippers—"

"No need," Noella said with a wave of dismissal.

"But—"

"They're yours, dear." She held her hand out to the girl bouncing at the foot of the bed. "Come, Ingrid, darling. Let's let Ella get some rest. We should be docking soon. You, too, Gustav."

Gustav unfolded his long body from the chair and limped toward the door. "Glad to see you awake, my lady."

Ingrid bounced off the end of the bed and took hold of Noella's hand. As they exited, Ingrid said, "Wasn't that the best adventure?"

Nicholas chuckled. "The moment we were on the ship, she perked up. She couldn't wait to tell anyone who listened about how we escaped the fortress."

"And all that time she seemed so terrified," Ella said.

"She seems happy to be going home. Honestly, I think my mother must have had something to do with her renewed state of mind."

"How do you mean?" Ella asked.

"I think she helped her forget the worst of it."

Ah, of course. Magic. Nicholas rose from the bed and walked across to a small table in the corner. He poured a steaming cup of tea and brought it to her. She took it, grateful.

"We'll return to the castle for a day or so to clean up and rest, then head back to the village to return her to her parents," he said.

"They must be so worried."

She thought of Agnes and Lukas and wondered how they were faring with the news of their granddaughter in Malvina's hands.

But she couldn't help but wonder what would happen to her then. Once they had returned Ingrid and—hopefully—the Christmas Star was repaired, then what? Was she to return to her own home with her vile stepmother and stepsisters? The thought made her stomach clench in terror.

How could she tell Nicholas she didn't want to go back? How could she tell him she wanted to stay here with him? And where would she live? What would she do?

She looked at him over the rim of her cup. He had a contemplative look on his handsome face, as though he had the same thoughts as she did. But he didn't voice them. And neither did she.

"Once we get back to the village," he said, "maybe you can help me repair the Christmas Star?"

Hope swelled deep inside her. "I would love that. But...how?"

He gave her a knee-melting smile. "We'll figure that out when we get there. Now, I'll let you rest and see if my mother can conjure you some proper footwear."

"I guess she really wasn't my fairy godmother," Ella said. A twinge of sadness went through her. If she wasn't her fairy godmother, though, why gift her with the slippers? And the gown and the ball?

"Oh, I wouldn't say that," he said.

"Why is that?"

He looked thoughtful for a long moment before he finally replied. "She saw something in you. Something magical and joyful and endearing. She *wanted* you to have those slippers. She picked you, Ella. If that doesn't make her your fairy godmother, I don't know what does."

With that, he left her alone to contemplate his words.

Ella looked at the glass slippers, wondering if he was right. Wondering if Alice was right about the legend of the shoes. Indeed, she did feel a certain power while wearing them. As though for the first time in her life, she was in control.

She noticed a hairline fracture on the toe of the right slipper. She must have damaged it when she tripped and fell. She slipped it off, then held it closer for inspection. Yes, there was definitely a faint crack in the glass. A pang of sadness went through her.

She clutched the shoe to her chest, gripping it tight. How could she possibly return to her previous life when so much had changed for her? She dreaded the thought of going back to her life of drudgery serving those wretched women. Truthfully, they didn't deserve her nor did she deserve a life of servitude to the three spoiled, unkind women who lived in her house.

Her house that was rightfully hers when her father passed. Not that she had any proof he was dead. Her gut, though, told her as much. He was never coming back. She doubted he would like to see her living in such a way. But what to do about it? She didn't have the means to evict her stepmother and stepsisters. Nor did she have money to find a new place to live.

She was stuck.

A swift knock on the door sounded, breaking her out of her dismal thoughts.

"Come in," she called.

Noella opened the door a crack and stuck in her head. "Ah, you're still awake. Good." She entered the room carrying a pair of boots. "Here you are, dear."

Ella took them. She took her other foot out of the slipper. Placing them beside her on the bed, she pulled on the boots.

"Thank you," she said.

"You're welcome, dear. You'll want those when we dock," she said. "When you feel up to it, come up on the deck."

Noella turned to leave.

"Noella," she called. The woman paused, giving her a questioning glance. Ella took a deep breath, then asked, "What happens now?"

"What do you mean?"

"I mean...to me. What happens to me now?"

She seemed genuinely perplexed by the question, as though it had never crossed her mind. "What do you want to happen?"

Ella chewed her lower lip, unsure how to answer. "I suppose I should return home?" It was more of a question testing Noella's reaction—to see if she would ask her to stay with them in Rovenheim.

A flash of disappointment went over her face before she managed to conceal it. "If that's your wish then of course we'll see to it. Whenever you're ready, dear."

Without waiting for a reply, she slipped out the door, closing it behind her. Though she had an answer, Ella frowned. What answer did she expect from Noella? That she would tell her to stay? Offer her a place in the castle?

Ella shrugged off the disappointment. There was no sense in wallowing in it. She would make the most of what time she had left with Nicholas and all the rest. She slid off the bed and headed to the deck, leaving the glass slippers behind.

CHAPTER 25

After they docked, Captain Bart and his crew saw them disembark. Gustav had already deboarded and was off securing their horses back to the castle. Ingrid bounced from one foot to the other, clearly having the time of her life.

As they said their farewells, the pirate took Ella's hand in his calloused one and bent to kiss it. Ingrid emitted a sigh as if it was the most romantic thing in the world. Ella stifled a chuckle.

"Farewell, my lady," he said, a twinkle in his eyes. "May your journey be swift and calm."

"Thank you, captain. And for the use of your cabin." Gently, she pulled her hand from his grasp, trying not to think about how rough his palm was against hers.

"It was my pleasure." He bowed with a flourish and Ella couldn't help but smile. "How's the ankle?"

She twisted her foot to show him she was fine. "Much better, thank you."

Nicholas handed over a purse heavy with gold. "Five hundred gold pieces, as per our agreement and a little extra for the heroics."

The pirate took the purse, holding it in his hands. He gave a nod of thanks. "My crew and I thank you, your highness. This will see us through the harsh winter and keep us fed until spring."

"I'm glad to hear it," Nicholas said.

Noella was next. "Captain Bart, thank you for your help. It was much appreciated."

He reached for her hand to kiss it, but she drew it back and gave him a jaunty wave instead. Next was Ingrid who was more than happy to allow the pirate to bow to her.

"Miss Ingrid, have a safe trip home," he said.

She waited, giving him an expectant look. He glanced from her to Ella who gave him an encouraging nod. Finally, he took Ingrid's hand in his and gave it a light kiss on the back if it. The girl blushed, her cheeks flaming. When he released her hand, a smile lit up her face.

"I can't wait to tell Mama and Papa I met a real pirate!" And then she bounded down the gangplank ahead of them, her boots thumping with every joyful step.

"She's a handful, that one," Captain Bart said. "Good luck getting her home."

Nicholas gave him a salute of farewell. Ella and Noella followed him off the ship to the dock, where Ingrid waited with Gustav and four horses.

When they paused on the dock, Noella turned to her son, her hands in fists on her hips. "You gave that pirate five hundred gold pieces?"

"It was his price and we needed to get to Ingrid," Nicholas said, unapologetically.

She heaved a sigh and cut a glance to the girl who was currently jabbering away at Gustav while he readied the horses.

"Well, since it was for a worthy cause..."

"It was, Mother." He kissed her cheek. "Where are you off to?"

She looked astonished. "What makes you think I'm off somewhere, hm?"

"There are only four horses," Ella pointed out, amused.

"Ah, so there is." She gave Ella a rueful smile. "I'm off to spread more good tidings and cheer. I'll see you off at the castle before you leave for the village."

Then she was gone in a cloud of glittery fairy dust.

"How many horses are at the castle? Do they all have names? What's your favorite color?" Ingrid chattered away at Gustav, who had an exhausted look on his face.

Ella smiled. "I suppose we should give poor Gustav a break and get going."

Nicholas watched with a bemused look on his face. "Let's make sure she rides next to him."

"Why is that?" Ella asked.

"So Ingrid can talk to him the whole way, of course." He flashed a wicked grin before going to his horse and sticking his foot into the stirrup.

Ella snickered. She limped to her horse, her ankle better but still a little sore. She climbed into the saddle. Meanwhile, Gustav helped Ingrid onto her horse.

"Do you know how to ride?" he asked.

"Of course, I do!" she said.

She snapped the reins. The horse took off at a full gallop, leaving the rest of them behind.

"I think you best catch her, Gustav," Nicholas said, amused.

Gustav muttered a curse under his breath, quickly mounted his horse and took off after the girl.

"This should be an amusing ride home," Nicholas said, watching the disappearing form of the Captain of the Guard. He nudged his horse into a walk.

"Poor Gustav." Ella nudged her horse with her heels falling in step with him.

"Poor Gustav nothing," Nicholas said. "He's getting a dose of his own medicine, I'd say."

Gustav finally caught up to the girl. He leaned close enough to grab the reins and slow her to a trot. She blushed, giving him an adoring look as he slowed them both down. He said something to her Ella couldn't hear and she nodded.

"Looks like he has an admirer," she said.

"He does," Nicholas said with a nod. His eyes landed on hers, a spark of some indefinable emotion there. "And so do you."

Now it was her turn to blush, the heat rushing to her cheeks. She looked away, turning her eyes forward and keeping her expression as neutral as possible. Her emotions were a jumbled mess, making it hard for her to think clearly. She didn't want to say something she would ultimately regret.

Like asking him if she could stay here in Rovenheim.

And so, she said nothing because she didn't know what to say.

As the day waned, the rest of the trip was uneventful. The only chatter came from Ingrid who was full of questions for Gustav. By the time they reached the castle stable, his face was lined with exhaustion from all the questions. Nicholas, however, was entertained by it all.

"This is where I tell you good night," Gustav said.

"You're leaving?" Ingrid looked as though she were losing her best friend.

"I have duties to attend." He gave her a deep bow. "Safe travels, my lady." Then he turned his attention to Ella. "And to you, too, my lady."

"Thank you, Gustav. Good night."

As he left them, Nicholas ushered them from the stable. "Let's get you settled, Ingrid."

She skipped ahead of him, her braids bouncing. It was the oddest thing to watch her. As if she had never experienced the trauma of being Malvina's prisoner. But then, Nicholas did say his mother had something to do with her renewed state of mind.

Alice was waiting for them when they arrived. Nicholas handed Ingrid off to her.

"Ingrid, this is Miss Alice. She has a nice cozy room for you."

As they walked away, Ingrid launched into a string of questions for Alice about the castle.

"How many people live here, Miss Alice? Is this really the home of the king and queen? Will I get to meet the king?"

Every time Alice tried to answer, Ingrid asked another question. Her eyes were bright and round and full of wonder, taking in everything and everyone as Alice escorted her up the winding staircase.

Ella was unable to contain the chuckle that erupted.

"And now, Miss Ella." Nicholas turned to her, grasping her hand in his. "Let's get you settled in for the night."

He led her back to the same bedchamber she had before they left. That lovely, spacious royal suite with the huge fireplace and the comfy bed. He pushed open the door and paused there, still holding her hand.

"Tomorrow we'll take Ingrid back to the village to her parents," he said.

"And repair the Christmas Star?" she asked.

He nodded. He searched her face, his eyes brimming with gentle contemplation. He glanced down at her lips before moving up again. "Then return you to your own realm."

It was to be tomorrow then, when she would return to her dismal life. She had only a few hours left to spend with him and most of that would be sleeping. Sadness crept through her. She tried her best to keep it at bay.

"Yes, I should return," she said. "Good night, Nicholas."

She took a step into the room, but he refused to release her hand. Turning back, she gave him a questioning look.

"Ella..." He paused as he chose his next words. His lips parted as he started to say something else, but then changed his mind.

"Yes?" she asked. Hope rose in her breast as she waited for him to continue.

He hesitated, started to say something and then gave her a weak smile. Instead, he said, "I hope you sleep well."

Then he released her hand and was gone.

CHAPTER 26

Ella curled in her bed, staring through the darkness unable to shake the disappointment that had flooded her when Nicholas left her. She was certain he was going to ask her to stay, but then changed his mind. Perhaps he thought she would refuse because she wanted to return to her previous life.

She'd kept most of the details to herself, because she didn't want to admit to him she was a servant in her own home. That her stepmother was a terrible person who squandered away all their money on frivolous things for herself and her daughters, never leaving enough for even the grocer. That her stepsisters were spoiled, selfish, and unkind.

She didn't want to tell him any of that because she didn't want his pity.

In hindsight, though, she wished she had told him everything. She wished she'd told him about her life back in Whitebridge.

If he'd asked her to stay, she would have said yes. She would have stayed. For him and Noella and all of them. It was as though she belonged here in this wintery world. Though she didn't know

Nicholas that well, she felt as though she belonged with him. He was her prince. Her true love. The one the slippers—

With a gasp, she sat straight up. Her heart palpitated with the sudden memory pounding into her. She'd left the glass slippers on the ship in Captain Bart's quarters.

How could she be so forgetful? She smacked her forehead with the palm of her hand.

And how was she going to get them back? Worse, how was she going to confess to Noella she'd left them behind?

Dread shifted through her, making her stomach clench into a tight knot. She flung off the bedcovers and padded to the window, shoving aside the curtains. It was still dark outside. There was no sense in sounding the alarm and waking everyone in the castle. Even so, that awful feeling would not go away.

Knowing she wouldn't sleep she plopped down in the wing-backed chair and curled her legs to the side to watch the dying embers of the fire. Her feet were cold, but it wasn't enough to spur her into action and find stockings. She clutched her elbows as she shivered. It was cold in her room, but she deserved to be cold as penance for leaving behind the glass slippers.

She must have drifted off to sleep because the next thing she knew, Alice was shaking her awake.

"My lady, are you well?"

Ella lifted her head, her neck aching from the awkward position. She rubbed the back of it and glanced around, confused. Then she recalled her terrible mistake and how, shaking from fear and the cold, she climbed into the chair to wait out the night.

"What time is it?" she muttered.

"It's morning. Did you sleep in that chair all night?"

"Not all night." Ella uncurled her numb legs and managed to stand. "I...I couldn't sleep."

"It's freezing in here." Alice added logs to the fire, stoked it, and got it going again.

Ella shivered, clutching her elbows. Morning light slashed through the uncovered window. The curtain was still shoved aside where Ella had left it. It had snowed overnight, leaving the ground covered in a thick, white blanket. Dust motes danced in the bright light.

"Let's get you dressed. You don't want to keep your prince waiting." Alice bustled about the room, gathering her warm clothes.

"I really don't think he's my prince," Ella said, still clutching her elbows.

"Why is that?" Alice bent to retrieve her boots from the side of the bed.

"Well...we don't know each other very well and—"

"Poppycock. I've seen the way he looks at you." She snatched up a pair of woolen stockings and handed them to Ella.

"How does he look at me?" A glimmer of hope trickled through her, but she refused to allow it to consume her.

Alice dropped her boots onto the floor at her feet, then picked up her wool dress. "He gives you adoring looks."

Her cheeks flushed hot. She turned away so Alice wouldn't see. Their one kiss suddenly popped into her mind, unbidden, which made her press her fingertips against her lips. His mouth was solid, sweet, tender. Thinking of it made her heart turn over and her stomach flutter.

"You don't agree?" Alice asked, when she didn't answer.

"I'm not sure."

"I've seen him with other girls," she said. "He's looked at none of them the way he looks at you."

Ella turned to face her finally, still holding the woolen stockings. Her brows drew together in question but she wasn't sure what she wanted to ask.

"It's true he's a bit of a rogue, but he's different around you," Alice continued.

"How?"

"Like he cares about you."

Hearing that gave her the heart squeeze and her knees threatened to buckle. She made her way to the bed and sat on the edge.

"He didn't care about the others?" Ella asked, her voice a rough whisper.

Alice took a seat next to Ella, reaching for her hand and squeezing it. "Not like he does about you."

Silence descended between them as Ella considered her words. If she was right, then perhaps there was a chance for her to stay with Nicholas. But if she asked and he refused...she would be crushed.

"By the way, where are the glass slippers? I don't see them anywhere."

And just like that, her hopes were dashed, replaced by her horrifying guilt. If she could go back in time and fix her mistake, she would. Her chest tightened and she flushed again, this time not because of her amorous feelings for the prince, but because she was embarrassed to admit the truth. Even to Alice.

"I...don't have them anymore."

"You don't?" The woman sounded perplexed.

Ella turned to her, reaching for her hands and grasping them hard in hers. "I made a terrible mistake. I'm terrified to admit it but even more terrified for Nicholas or his mother to find out."

The woman's brows drew together. "Now, now, dear. It can't be all that bad. What is it?"

"We sailed back from Malvina's fortress and, well, I left the slippers behind on the ship. I forgot them." She released one of the woman's hands and pressed cold fingertips against her forehead. "I can't believe I forgot them."

Alice patted her shoulder. "It's not the end of the world. I'm sure Noella can get them back."

"But she trusted me with them and I let her down." Her voice wavered. Tears threatened, burning the back of her throat.

Alice scooted closer to her on the bed and wrapped an arm around her shoulders. "Is there anything I can do to help?"

She shook her head. "I don't think so, but thank you for letting me tell you." She looked up through her lashes at the woman. "You won't tell anyone?"

A small smile crossed her lips. "It will be our secret." Then she squeezed her tight. "Come now. Let's get you dressed."

Alice kept her promise and didn't breathe a word to anyone about Ella's confession. After she helped her dress, Ella headed out of the royal suite to meet the others in the grand foyer. Nicholas and Noella were in a deep conversation. Next to them, Ingrid swirled her skirts and took in all her surroundings. The young girl was dressed in a fresh gown, her hair washed and combed and re-braided, and her face bright and shining and smiling. As soon as she saw Ella, she bounded to her and flung herself into her arms with a giant hug. It was as if the girl hadn't seen her in ages when in truth it had only been a few hours.

Ella hugged her back. "Are you happy to be going home?"

Ingrid nodded. "Yes. Ella, did you know I had a room all to myself? At home, I have to share with my sister." She wrinkled her nose in distaste. "I can't wait to tell Freya all about it!"

"There you are, dear."

Noella bustled up, as if noticing her for the first time. Her silver hair hung loose about her shoulders in waves. She wore a green velvet gown with a gold and silver belt. The sleeves came to a point on the top of her hands. Silver earbobs in the shape of snowflakes dangled from each ear. Every time Ella saw her, she looked elegant and refined.

"You look tired. Did you sleep well?"

"Not so much," Ella admitted.

"Was your bed uncomfortable? Did my son give you less than adequate chambers?" She spun to face him, her tone sounding motherly. "Nicholas—"

"She was in the royal suite next to me, Mother," he said, sounding weary.

Noella turned back to her. "Is that true?"

"Yes. I just had a hard time sleeping. Noella, there's something I need to tell you—"

"The horses are saddled and ready," Gustav announced as he made his entrance.

When Ingrid saw him, she bounced away from Ella and headed right for him. She fluttered her lashes at him as she looked up at him with rapt adoration. "Hi, Gustav."

He dropped to her level, smiling, and spoke to her, telling her all about the horse she would ride into town. Ingrid listened, attentive to his every word.

Noella blinked surprise. "It appears our dashing Captain of the Guard has an admirer."

"He does," Ella said with a nod. "Noella—"

"You should be going." Noella bustled away from her and back to her son. "There's a storm brewing. We're due for a lot of snow this evening. If you don't make it back before nightfall, you may have to spend the night in the village."

"We'll be on our way, then," Nicholas said.

"Are you coming, too, Gustav?" Ingrid asked.

"Not this time."

Her face fell in disappointment.

"But..." he added, "perhaps I'll see you in the village sometime."

"You'll come visit me?" She blinked up at him, a hopeful look on her cherub face.

"If I can." He gave her a knee-melting smile.

"Safe travels, dear." Noella kissed Nicholas on the cheek, then turned to Ingrid. She reached into her pocket and pulled out a blue velvet box. "And this is for you."

"For me?" She took the box and opened it. Nestled inside the box, was a necklace with a tiny snowflake that looked much like Noella's earbobs. Ingrid gave a little gasp.

"To remember us," Noella said with a smile. Her blue eyes twinkled.

"Thank you," Ingrid breathed. "I will wear it always." She paused, then looked back up at the queen of Rovenheim, her face splitting into a broad smile. "And Freya will be *so* jealous!"

"Now, now," Noella said. "That's not nice." She reached into her other pocket and brought out two more little boxes, one square and one long and narrow. "This one is for her." She handed her the square box. "And this is for your brother." Then gave her the long narrow box.

"They will be *so* surprised!" Ingrid amended.

They all laughed as Ingrid pocketed the gifts.

When all the final farewells were made, Noella was gone in a puff of magic once again. She never stayed in one place any length of time.

And Ella still did not have a chance to confess. She glanced at Nicholas who was leading Ingrid away toward the stables. Gustav stepped up next to her and held out his arm.

"Shall I escort you, my lady?"

Ella eyed it and then gave him a slight grin. "Won't Ingrid be jealous?"

"I don't think she'll mind." He nodded in her direction.

Nicholas held the girl's hand as they walked and she chattered nonstop. He made the appropriate responses when she paused to take a breath. Ella giggled.

"In that case, you shall."

She took his arm and together they walked to the stables.

CHAPTER 27

The return to the village was a shorter trip than when she and Nicholas initially left. They were on foot then. She was grateful for the horse now, especially since there was a foot of snow on the ground and flakes continued to trickle down from the wintery sky.

Ingrid chatted along the way, talking about her family. She had a younger sister, Freya, and a brother, Ivar. Her father was the town apothecary. Everyone knew him and their family. They lived in a small house on the outskirts, likely near Agnes and Lukas, her grandparents. She wanted a dog and had asked for one for Christmas. She was young and cheerful and loved to read fairy tales by the fire. She insisted having a dog would make her life much better.

As they arrived at the village gates, something was awry. Nicholas stiffened in the saddle, then, without warning, kicked his mount into a full gallop. She and Ingrid exchanged a curious look.

"What is it?" the girl asked.

"Something's wrong," Ella said. "Let's hurry."

She nudged her horse into a trot. Ingrid did the same. When they arrived at the gates, Nicholas dismounted and walked several steps into the village. Ella and Ingrid came to a halt and also dismounted. She followed him inside the gates.

There was an eerie silence. The village was deserted.

"I don't understand," he said. "It should be bustling with activity this time of year."

On the other side of the village, though, the enormous tree stood dark. No lights twinkled like they had when Ella first arrived. The festive atmosphere was gone. The shops were closed and dark.

"This is Malvina's doing," he said, his breath pluming white in front of him. "Because she destroyed the Christmas Star."

Ingrid stood between them and shuddered. She ran to her father's shop. She tried the knob, but the door was locked. A closed sign was in the window. She cupped her face to peer inside it, then turned around, dejected.

"There's no one there."

"Perhaps we should take Ingrid to her home. Maybe her parents can tell us what's happened," Ella said.

Nicholas nodded. "That's a good idea."

Ingrid gave directions to her house. They returned to the horses, mounted, and then rode through the desolate village. Seeing the dark tree sent a pang of sorrow through Ella. As they passed by it, though, she saw the sparkling shards of the Christmas Star at the foot of it. Discarded. It gave her an idea. Once they delivered Ingrid safely to her parents, they could return and try to put the pieces back together.

It was a short ride to her home. The small cottage had one chimney with gray smoke curling out of it. A wood fence wrapped around the front yard. Snow heaped on the pickets. As they approached, Ingrid's face broke into a joyful grin. She pulled her horse to a stop, jumped down from the saddle, and ran the rest of the way, her braids flopping behind her.

Ella and Nicholas both halted several feet from the gate. Ingrid burst through the front door, calling for her parents. Then there was silence. Relief sputtered through Ella knowing they had returned her home safely.

"Well..." Nicholas said. "I suppose our duty has been fulfilled."

She nodded. "I suppose it has."

"We should return to the castle before nightfall. My mother said a winter storm was coming."

Her heart picked up speed, drumming hard in her chest. She tried not to read too much into the *we* of his statement.

"We should," she agreed, her voice hoarse in the cold late morning air.

Nicholas turned his horse. Ella started to do the same, but as she did, Ingrid rushed out of the front door dragging a woman behind her. A man followed along with a girl and a boy. An older couple trailed after the two younger children. Agnes and Lukas.

Ingrid's parents and siblings and grandparents.

Happiness shot through Ella seeing the reunited family, the smiles on their faces, the pure joy and relief at having their eldest returned.

"Nicholas, wait," she said, her voice urgent.

He halted, turned back, and saw them all emerging.

"Wait!" Ingrid called, waving her hand in a giant wave. "I want you to meet my family!"

Ella hopped down from the saddle, her steps quick as she hurried to meet them. Nicholas was right behind her.

"But we've already met." Agnes stepped around the others and headed right for Ella. She caught her in a fierce hug, squeezing her tight. When she pulled back, her face was bright with a smile. "Ella, I'm so happy to see you."

"Hello, Agnes. I'm happy to see you, too."

"You know each other?" Nicholas asked.

She nodded. "Yes. Agnes and Lukas took me in when I, ah, arrived."

Ingrid's mother bustled forward, then, pushing aside Agnes. She was tall, with long hair the same color as her daughters, pulled back and tied with a leather thong at the nape of her neck. She wore an apron over her woolen gown as though she had been in the middle of cooking and dropped everything when Ingrid arrived. There were tears in her pale green eyes. Tears of joy and relief and gratitude. She wrapped her arms around Ella, pulling her tight.

"Thank you. Thank you so much," she breathed in Ella's ear.

Ella squeezed her back, so happy for her and the rest of the family. When the woman pulled back, she held her at arm's length, unable to stop smiling.

"You don't know how worried we were and how grateful we are to have her back unharmed," the woman said.

"We were happy to do it," Nicholas said.

"Mama, this is the crown prince. I *told* you I met the prince! And the queen! And look. The queen gave me this necklace." She fingered the tiny snowflake, showing her mother.

Her mother chuckled, then cut a glance at Nicholas. "Forgive us, your highness. We didn't quite believe her when she said the Prince of Rovenheim and his lady brought her home."

Ella flushed hot as she snuck a glance at Nicholas. He stepped forward, gave a bow to the woman.

"It was my lady's idea to rescue Ingrid from the fortress." Nicholas flashed Ella a smile, cheerfully giving her all the credit for their quest.

"Your highness, we forget our manners," the man said. "Won't you come inside for some tea?" He motioned to the still open door.

"We should return—" Nicholas began.

But Ingrid went to him, grasping his hand and gazing up at him with pleading eyes. "Please, Nicholas? Then you can help me tell them all about our grand adventure."

Her mother lifted a brow, giving her daughter a sideways glance. "It was a grand adventure? To be kidnapped?"

"I'm sure the prince and his lady have far more important things to do than regale us with fairy tales, Ingrid," her father said.

"It's not a fairy tale, Papa! It's the truth."

Ella cleared her throat and stepped up next to Nicholas. "Perhaps we could stay for a pot of tea." She made a show of shivering. "It's a bit damp and cold out here and we've been riding for a long time."

Nicholas gave her sideways glance. She flashed a smile and shrugged. Finally, he turned back to them.

"All right. I suppose we can stay for some tea."

"And lemon cakes!" Ingrid added.

Then she skipped back into the house. Her sister, Freya, whispered loud enough for all to hear, "Did you really meet a pirate?"

***

Ella sat curled in the well-worn oversized chair with her legs curled under her while she held a cup of steaming tea under her nose. Her belly was full of beef stew and lemon cakes, leaving her feeling drowsy and comfortable and deliriously happy.

Before dinner, Lars had seen to their horses. He put them in his stable for the night and made sure they were fed and watered.

Now, Ingrid stood in front of the fireplace, telling her tale of rescue and escape, using all sorts of hand and arm gestures, while her parents and siblings listened in captivated silence.

Her parents, Lars and Ava, cuddled on the sofa. Freya perched on her mother's lap. Ivar sat cross-legged on the floor looking up at his sister with wide-eyed wonder. Agnes and Lukas had excused themselves after dinner to return home.

Ella glanced at Nicholas, who sat in the chair across from her. Light smoldered in his deep blue eyes. Her heart turned over as he gave her a small, tired smile. She had a bit of guilt for talking him into staying, but he didn't seem to mind nor did his appetite.

Ingrid's favorite part was when Nicholas carried her to the gate after she'd sprained her ankle. She seemed to think that was the most romantic thing ever, making Ella blush to the roots of her hair. She pretended not to be affected by it by taking a sip of her tea.

"That's quite a tale," her father said.

"OH! I almost forgot." Ingrid reached into her pocket and brought out the two boxes Noella gave her. She handed them to her siblings.

Freya's eyes lit up when she opened the square box and pulled out the snowflake necklace that matched her sister's. Ivar opened his to find a cloak pin in the shape of the famous Christmas Star that sat atop the giant tree in the village square.

"My goodness," Ava breathed when she saw the gifts. Tears sparkled in her eyes as she looked at Nicholas. "Please convey our heartfelt thanks to the queen."

He gave a nod. "I will." Then he addressed Lars, "Why is the village deserted?"

Lars and Ava exchanged a glance. Ava set Freya on her feet and rose.

"Come, children. It's time for bed."

"But I'm not tired," Ivar said, yawning.

She ushered them out of the room, but Ingrid turned and dashed back to Ella. She flung herself into her lap, slipping her arms around her neck and hugging her tight.

"I hope you marry the prince," she whispered. Then she released her and hurried away with her mother and siblings.

Ella flushed, feeling the heat crawling up her neck. Her body was heavy and warm. She watched the others walk away, and did her best to avoid looking at Nicholas. She feared if she did, she would ask to stay with him.

Once Ava and the children were out of the room, Lars got to his feet. He stoked the dying fire, coaxing the flames back to life.

"Things changed when Malvina destroyed the Christmas Star." He faced the fireplace, the yellow-orange light flickering over his bearded face.

Nicholas leaned forward, his elbows on his knees. "Changed, how?"

"People stopped coming to the village to shop. The mayor canceled the rest of the festivities. I'd already closed my shop when Ingrid was taken, but since the star was destroyed..." He paused, turned to face them. "It was as though all the joy of the season was destroyed, too."

"There must be a way to repair it," Ella said, thinking of the shards of the broken Star at the base of the tree.

Lars shook his head. "I know not. Only that...things are different. Quiet. Sad. Malvina's attack left everyone terrified she would return and obliterate the village itself. The mayor thought it best to shut everything down. With Ingrid taken and the Star in pieces, it seemed like the best course of action."

"The mayor was wrong," Ella said, her words more vehement than she meant for them to be.

Nicholas gave her a surprised look as he glanced at her.

She uncurled her legs and stood, still clutching the tea cup, the porcelain warm in her hand. "There has to be some way to bring back the joy and festivities to the village."

"Without the Christmas Star?" Lars gave her a doubtful look.

"Yes."

"Do you have an idea, Ella?" Nicholas asked.

His intense gaze was on her. He, too, rose and their eyes met. His twinkling and full of life and hope. And something more. Something tender that made her heart turn over.

"I do. I want to return to village to see if we can repair the Star."

"Well, I'm afraid you'll have to wait until morning," Lars said. "It's full dark and snowing quite hard."

Ella glanced at the window with the parted curtain and saw he was correct. Snow came down in thick blankets of white.

"I'm afraid we're stuck here," Nicholas said.

Lars grinned. "That's all right. We have a place you can stay."

"I'll take the sofa," Nicholas said.

As if it was the most natural thing in the world for the Crown Prince of Rovenheim to sleep on someone's sofa.

Ella didn't miss the look of shock that plastered Lars's face.

"But, your highness—"

"I insist." He held up a hand to halt any more objections. "We've already inconvenienced you enough."

"It's no inconvenience, I assure you. It's an honor to have you and your lady under our roof."

Another blush. If Ella didn't stop blushing every time she was called *his lady*, her face was going to light on fire.

"Still, I'll take the sofa."

"If you insist, your highness. I'll have my wife bring you blankets."

"Thank you, Lars." When he looked at her, the wild blue depths of his eyes spoke to her in a way that made her gut clench into a tight knot. "Good night, Ella."

It was a simple phrase. One that didn't mean anything other than what he said. But the way he looked at her, the way he spoke to her, made her mind think it meant *more*.

"Good night, your highness."

Though she had been using his given name, she didn't want to seem too forward in front of their host. She followed Lars to the back of the cottage where there was a spare room with two double beds. An oil lamp burned brightly on the table in between them. The room décor was definitely that of two young girls.

"I hope you find this room comfortable."

"Is this the girls' room?" she asked.

"Yes, but, they'll be sleeping with us tonight."

"Oh, I couldn't take their room."

His face softened as he smiled. "I assure you they think it's a grand thing to have the prince's lady spend the night in their room."

"But—" started to protest again.

"Sleep well, my lady."

He gave her a nod of goodnight as he closed the door behind him.

CHAPTER 28

Another sleepless night passed her by. Ella spent most of it staring at the ceiling in the narrow bed, thinking about everything from Nicholas to what would happen to her when she returned home. How would her stepmother treat her *then*? And her stepsisters? They were positively vile. It was fruitless to obsess over what had not occurred, and yet she had a difficult time shoving those thoughts away.

Even the bed she was in now was far more comfortable than the lumpy one back home. The blankets were thick and warm and cozy. At home, the blankets were thin and threadbare and didn't do much to keep her warm from the cold winter nights. Here, the house was full of love and life and laughter. There, the house was full of animosity and orders and endless back-breaking chores.

It was almost as though the people of Rovenheim—Ingrid and Agnes, Nicholas and Noella, even Gustav—had become her family. They treated her with kindness and respect instead of loathing and contempt.

Her heart ached. A deep-seated ache that throbbed through her at the thought of leaving it all behind.

She rolled to her side, trying to ignore the crush of tears that wanted to erupt. Trying to pretend that everything was fine and once they repaired the Christmas Star, she would return home to the life she had before. A life of utter desolation and loneliness.

When the morning light slashed through the one window in the room, she shoved off the bedclothes and dressed. She was grateful for the thick stockings, the boots, the woolen gown and the cloak in which Alice had outfitted her. It would make riding back into the village in the thick snow bearable.

As she exited the room, she heard cheerful, chattering voices and paused a moment to take it in. Nicholas was talking to Ingrid and Freya and telling them a grand story about a fire-breathing dragon that once lived in the Grimbrande Mountains and had, eventually, taken the form of Malvina. That's why she was so mean because, deep down, she was a dragon. They laughed, knowing he jested. Even Ella smiled at the story.

Then she heard Ava calling them in to breakfast. And the shuffling of feet as they headed into the kitchen. She smelled the fatty scent of fried bacon, a twang of sausage, and possibly oatcakes, and her stomach rumbled.

She headed into the kitchen, saw them gathering around the table. All of them. Nicholas on one side flanked by Freya and Ingrid. Ava on one end. Lars on the other. Ivar opposite the prince and the girls with an empty seat next to him.

For her.

It was all too much. Overcome with emotion, she dashed through the cottage, heading right for the front door, tears burning her eyes. Nicholas called her name but she refused to look his way as she pulled open the door and stepped into the bright, frigid morning. The cold wind stung her cheeks and froze the tears in her eyes. She whisked them away as she stared across the expanse of white lawn at the picket fence. In the distance, a dog barked.

The door behind her opened and closed with a soft snick. She stiffened, blinking away the tears and taking a deep breath to steady herself.

"Ella? Are you all right?" Nicholas was behind her. Probably standing at the door wondering why she had run out of the cottage.

"Yes." She plastered on her best smile and spun to face him. "I'm fine. It's just that... it's morning already and we have a Christmas Star to repair and I have to..." Her words trailed off.

His face remained impassive, but she saw the drop of his shoulders. It was imperceptible. She would have missed it if she hadn't been looking.

"And then you have to return home. I'm sure you're ready. I'll get the horses."

He was so wrong, but she didn't correct him. If there was ever a time to tell him the truth—that she didn't want to go home, that she'd left the glass slippers on the ship—now was the time. But words froze in her throat.

He returned inside, likely to tell Lars they were ready to depart. Moments later, Nicholas led the two mounts around the end of the house, their hooves crunching in the snow.

"Shall we?" He gave her a faint smile. A faint *fake* smile. As though he had something he wanted to say but was afraid to say it.

Like her.

She nodded, sticking her foot into the stirrup and hoisting herself into the saddle. Her throat constricted with unshed tears, but she managed to swallow past the lump. Together, they rode from Ingrid's cottage back to the village, which wasn't far, though they had to take it slow because the thick snow blanketing the ground. The horses picked their way through it until, finally, the gate of the village came into view with the faded sign welcoming them to Rovenheim Village.

They left their horses at the gate, dismounted and entered.

Ella took the lead. She headed right for the tree where she saw the shards of the Star. The pieces were covered by the freshly fallen snow. She dropped to her knees and started digging, looking for the pieces.

"What are you looking for?" he asked.

"Yesterday, when we rode past the tree, I saw the shards of the Star on the ground here. But the snow covered them up."

He dropped down next to her and started to dig, helping her move the wet, sticky snow out of the way. Their hands bumped, her skin tingling even through her thick gloves. Their eyes met for a brief moment before they went back to digging. Both of them paused when they saw the first glittering piece.

"There," she said, her breath pluming white.

"I see it."

They went back to digging and finally uncovered the pieces. Nicholas picked them up, one by one. Ella noticed, though, not all the pieces were there. He held the biggest ones. The smaller pieces were missing.

"I don't think we can put it back together." He frowned down at the shards in his palms.

"We can try," she suggested.

As their eyes met, a look of bewilderment crossed his face. "How? When so many of the pieces are missing?"

She peered down at the gold fragments in his hands. Something occurred to her. Some of them looked as though they fit together. She started arranging them until it was clear what was missing. Their heads were bent together. He watched her intently as she moved one fragment next to another. The Star was almost whole again save for a few bits they were unable to find.

"There, you see," she said.

"There are still gaps," he said.

She placed her hands over his, covering what was left of the Star. "I know." She blew out a breath. "The Star represents more than just an object, though."

In the blue depths of his eyes, she saw despair over the loss of the ornament. But it was more than that.

"How do you mean?"

"I mean...it represents joy and hope and kindness. A sort of giving spirit. It brings happiness to all those who see it glittering and twinkling on top of the tree."

"But without it, there is none of that."

"I disagree," she said. "I believe it can still bring all those things, even if it *is* in pieces. This time of year is not about *things*. It's about people and how they make us feel. It's about a sense of hope and love. It's about being selfless and wanting to do special things for the people we love. We all still have those things without the Star. We have them here." She lifted her hand and placed it on his chest. She was aware of the faint beat of his heart against her palm.

"You are those things, Nicholas. You are hope and love and compassion for your people. I saw it in the faces of Lars and Ava and their children. I saw it in the faces of the people who live in your castle. Both you and Noella spread the spirit to all of them, even though you may not realize it."

"Ella..." He breathed her name, his breath white smoke between them.

He tipped his head to one side, his lips slightly parting. She knew what he meant to do and she wanted it. Her eyes fluttered closed in anticipation.

There, at the base of the massive Christmas tree, with the shards of the Star in his palms and her hand over his heart, he kissed her. His lips were cold but soft as they met hers, making her heart soar with elation. Her pulse raced. Her mind took in every detail because she never wanted to forget that magical moment.

As they kissed, a yellowish bright light flashed between them. He pulled back. She opened her eyes, fighting away the disappointment the kiss was over.

"Ella, look." His voice was a rough whisper.

She tore her eyes from his and glanced down. In his palm, was the shining Christmas Star and it was whole again.

"You did it," he said, admiration and adoration in his tone.

"I...I don't understand how."

"Because you have the Spirit of Christmas inside you, dear."

Noella's voice made them both jump. Ella dropped her hand from his chest. They both got to their feet and turned to face his mother, the queen. She wore a winter white gown with a brocade pattern in snowflakes, the edges trimmed in fur, and a matching cloak. A sprig of holly was pinned in her hair that was piled high on her head with ringlets framing her lovely, aged face. Her bright blue eyes twinkled with happiness and her red lips were curved in a smile.

"Mother, you really should announce yourself when you arrive. How long were you there, anyway?"

"Long enough."

She said it in a sing-song voice which made Ella think she'd been there all along and heard her speech. Her booted feet crunched on the snow as she approached and peered down at the shining Star in his hands.

"Nicely done." She sounded impressed.

Then she used her magic wand to lift it with a spray of magic. Higher and higher it went until finally it rested on the top of the tree. She gave her wand one last shake, lighting the rest of the tree in tiny twinkle lights.

"It's beautiful," Ella said.

"Of course, it is. You made it possible," Noella said.

"I helped," Nicholas said, sounding a bit vexed.

Noella patted his shoulder. "You were a bit disheartened about the Star. Come now, if it hadn't been for Ella, it would never be repaired."

When he frowned, his mother gave him a cheeky grin. Ella stifled a snicker.

"Now, then. I'm off to find the mayor and tell him the good news." She disappeared in a puff of magic.

Before either of them could move, she popped back in.

"I almost forgot." She reached into her pocket and pulled out a small vial with a cork. Inside was a shimmering substance. "This will send you home, Ella. When you're ready, pull off the cork and sprinkle a bit around you, then think of home."

Ella, her hands shaking, took it from Noella. "Thank you."

And she was gone in a puff of fairy dust once again.

Nicholas remained rooted to his spot, staring at the space his mother vacated. His face was unreadable. Ella clutched the vial in her gloved hand, staring down at it with her heart in her throat. This was it. Her way home, which meant her adventure with Nicholas had finally ended. Finally, he turned to her and reached for her free hand. He grasped it in his, squeezing it.

"Well," she said, searching for the right words. "I guess this is it."

"Your stepmother will want to know you're safe. I'm sure she's been worried about you," he said.

Ella doubted that, but said nothing. Her stepmother likely only missed her servitude. She gave him a weak smile and a nod. Tears threatened again but she blinked them away. There would be time to break down when she returned home.

She didn't ask anything silly like would she ever see him again. Instead, she took a deep breath and pulled the cork off the vial. He squeezed her hand once more.

"Goodbye, Ella."

She sniffed, her throat constricting. "Goodbye, Nicholas."

She sprinkled the shimmering fairy dust around her, closed her eyes, and thought of home. She no longer felt his hand on hers as the ground dropped out beneath her feet. Everything whirled around her. A whoosh of air went around her, stealing her breath and then she landed on the hard, cold ground.

She opened her eyes to darkness and saw she was outside the kitchen door of her childhood home. She'd left Rovenheim and Nicholas behind. Curling in on herself, she tucked her knees to her chest and burst into tears.

CHAPTER 29

W hen the first bird chirped, Ella peeled herself off the cold ground covered in a dusting of snow. The sun began to peek over the horizon and soon the day would come. In the distance, the clock tower from Whitebridge Palace clanged six times telling her the hour. She brushed her palms down her skirt, then smoothed her hair. She was, at least, still dressed in the wool dress and cloak from Rovenheim. On the ground at her feet was the empty vial. She bent to pick it up. It was the only thing she had to remember Noella and Nicholas.

With a resigned sigh, she pulled open the back door and stepped into the kitchen. She halted in the doorway, gaping at the utter disaster before her.

The fireplace was cold and dark, ashes piled under the grate. Dirty dishes littered the table in the center of the room. Dust covered every inch of countertop. The cupboard doors stood open, the contents empty. Even the floor was dirty. It was enough to make her want to walk away forever and never look back.

She shuddered to think what the rest of the house looked like if the kitchen was this bad.

There was no sense in standing around feeling sorry for herself. Taking a deep breath, she pulled off her cloak and hung it by the door. Then she shoved up the sleeves of her gown and got to work.

She needed water from the well to start washing dishes. She found the discarded pail by the backdoor and snatched it up. With every step outside to the well, her ire rose. How could they have allowed the kitchen to get into such a state? And if the cupboards were bare, what were they surviving on?

After retrieving water, she headed back inside to build a fire. She couldn't wash dishes with cold water. But there was no wood in the firewood rack. Back outside, she found a small stack by the shed. As she grabbed a few, she halted and peered around the yard. It suddenly occurred to her there were no animals. No chickens. No dog. An eerie sensation went over her.

Back inside, she dropped the logs, the fire forgotten. She had to see what was going on in the rest of the house. She pushed through the kitchen door and froze.

The house was a disaster. Dust coated every surface. All the silver was tarnished. Trash littered the floor. Furniture was either missing or tipped over.

What day was it? How long had she been gone?

On the dining table was a discarded newspaper with the headline announcing the royal Christmas ball. The ball in which she'd met and danced with Nicholas. Next to it, a paper announcing the wedding of the crown prince with a circular tea stain splotched across the story. The newspaper was dated one week after the ball.

With her heart in her throat, she hurried through to the stairs and ascended. The bedroom doors were closed. At the top of the stairs, she hesitated, shaking from head to toe. The house was silent.

Thinking of her own third-floor room, she rushed up the stairs, flung open the door and halted. Everything was as she left it. The shabby curtains at the window. The few Christmas decorations she had managed to use including the tiny star on top of the tree. The lumpy bed. She sagged against the doorframe, suddenly relieved to see her mother's decorations still in place. At least they hadn't taken that from her.

Back downstairs, she went to her stepmother's bedroom and knocked.

There was no response.

She gripped the knob in her sweating hand and turned, pushing it open a crack to peer inside.

The room was empty. She flung open the door open and stepped inside. The bed was still unmade, the blankets rumpled as if her stepmother rose that morning and decided to leave the house. There were still a few gowns in the wardrobe.

Next, she checked her stepsisters' bedroom. Also empty with rumpled beds.

The house was deserted for now, but the clothes left behind indicated they would be back.

She pressed her cold, shaking fingers to her lips.

All that time in Rovenheim she worried about returning to her stepmother, to her outrage that she had been gone for...well, she didn't know for how long. A week, possibly longer. Relief sputtered through her at the thought that she was gone. But was she gone for good? And if not, then for how long?

Her relief was short-lived when she realized she had no money and no means to take care of the house or the upkeep. How would she survive?

Her stomach rumbled. Back downstairs, she rummaged through the kitchen looking for any scrap of food. There was nothing. No eggs, no flour, not even tea. She cut a glance at her cloak hanging by the backdoor and decided to walk to the market.

The market was a bustle of activity. She paused at the entrance, taking it all in. All the holiday decorations had been removed, so she assumed the festivities had passed. The Christmas ball had been planned a few weeks before the holiday. It was her only point of reference.

With her stomach rumbling again, she headed to the grocer in the hopes Mr. Gibson would take pity on her and let her buy food and put it on their account. She had no idea if her wretched stepmother managed to pay the bill or not and guilt swarmed through her as she remembered her promise to the man she'd pay up by the end of the week.

That was before she'd disappeared to Rovenheim.

The bell tinkled as she entered the store, the basket on her arm. She approached the counter where Mr. Gibson was finishing up with a customer. As the woman took her purchase, she turned toward Ella. She recognized her as Mrs. FitzGerald who lived a few doors down from them. The woman's eyes flew open with shock.

"Ella? Ella Tremaine?" she asked.

"Yes?"

"Where have you been?" Mrs. FitzGerald asked.

"Uh…" She wasn't sure how to answer.

Mr. Gibson bustled around the end of the counter. He swept Ella into a fierce hug. "When we learned you disappeared, we all feared the worst."

He pulled back, holding her at arm's length and looking her over. "Are you well?"

"I'm fine. I was…out of town," she said, stumbling over her words.

"Well, your stepmother sure had no information about that," Mrs. FitzGerald said, sounding indignant. "She said you ran off. Didn't seem at all concerned about your whereabouts."

Ella cringed. That sounded like her stepmother.

"We all knew you didn't, though," Mr. Gibson said. "We feared she'd done something to you."

Her brows grew together. "What do you mean?"

"I think what Mr. Gibson is trying to say is," Mrs. FitzGerald added, "that no one trusts that Lillian Tremain *or* her wretched daughters." She sniffed derision to punctuate exactly what she thought of the woman.

"She'd tried to hire another servant, but no one would work for her," Mr. Gibson added. "We all know what sort of disposition the woman has. She's..." he paused, cleared his throat, "difficult."

And now that Ella was back, they had their servant back.

"And now she's remarried and has been on holiday for the last two weeks," Mrs. FitzGerald said.

"Remarried?" The word trickled out of her on a rough whisper.

"A rich fellow," Mr. Gibson said. "Named Livingstone."

Ella couldn't quite contain the shock rolling through her as she took in all the news.

"Word is he intends to hire a few servants once they return," Mr. Gibson said.

Mrs. FitzGerald snorted. "Ha. I doubt even *he* can get anyone to work for *that woman.* Sorry to run, but I must be on my way. Ella, I'm glad to see you. If you need anything, please do come see me. I'm only a few doors down."

Ella nodded as the woman waved farewell and exited the shop. Mr. Gibson put his hands on his hips, still giving her a good once over. He noticed her basket then.

"Apologies, Ella. You came in for groceries, not for the local gossip. What can I get you?"

Truthfully, Ella was glad for the local gossip. It gave her the information she needed when—and if—her stepmother and her new husband returned from their travels. It would also give her time to clean the house from top to bottom.

"I'm sorry I didn't come in to pay the bill—" she started.

"Mr. Livingstone paid it in full," he interrupted, waving away the thought as he headed back behind the counter.

So, Lillian Tremain—now Livingstone—managed to find herself a rich husband to pay all her debts. The ones she created using her father's money, while still living in her father's house. She tried her best to squelch the anger that rose in her, but it was difficult. She pressed her lips together in a thin line.

"I see."

He sensed her ire and gave her a small smile. "So, what can I get you?" Then he leaned forward and whispered, "and make sure all the items are *expensive.*"

Ella returned with so much food, she needed another basket to carry it all. Sugar, flour, tea, potatoes, carrots, bread, eggs, and even a slab of lean beef.

Once she was back home and all the items were unloaded and put away, she set to work cleaning the kitchen. She built a fire, brewed some tea, washed all the dishes and put them away. Then swept, mopped, and dusted. Finally, she was able to pause long enough to make her a light dinner.

By then, she was exhausted. The sun had started to set. She remained in the chair at the old, scarred, table with a cup of tea watching the fire flicker. Where was Nicholas? Was he missing her? She certainly hoped so. She missed him terribly.

She moved from the table to stoke the fire, sitting on her knees. Her lids grew heavy. The thought of walking up three flights of stairs to her room seemed daunting. She pillowed her head on her arms, watching the flames and, moments later, was fast asleep.

Nicholas sat alone in the wing-backed chair in his royal bedchamber with his legs stretched out in front of him brooding. The cup of tea he held had long since gone cold and he didn't have the energy to move and get a fresh one.

Every day since Ella left had been a day of misery. Ten days. He'd counted.

He wanted to ask her to stay with him, but she had looked so sad he assumed she was desperately homesick. She'd disappeared so quickly with the fairy dust his mother gave her, there was no prolonged farewell.

Perhaps that was for the best.

The holiday season was officially over. His father, the king, had returned from his worldly travels. His mother was also in residence, her task of spreading the Spirit of Christmas at last complete. Though he tried to enjoy the holiday with his family, there was definitely something missing. He had a hole in his heart. A hole only Ella could fill.

A sharp knock on his door interrupted his gloominess. Without waiting for him to grant entrance, the door opened and his mother bustled in. Her silvery hair hung in long, messy waves about her face with a pinched expression.

"I've just had a message," she announced without preamble. She paused for dramatic effect. "From Captain Bart."

He turned away from the fireplace and peered at his mother. She stood with her hands on her hips looking defiant.

"And?" he asked.

"He says he found a pair of delicate glass slippers in his quarters and wondered what to do with them. He finally decided they must have belonged to the 'girl with the luminous eyes,'" she put quotes around *the girl with the luminous eyes.* "Nicholas, she left them behind."

"I'm sure it wasn't on purpose, Mother."

"Well, you have to take them back to her."

He jumped to his feet. "I will do no such thing."

He marched across the room, eyeing the teapot. She followed. "Why not?"

"Because she doesn't want to see me."

"Poppycock!" she said and then huffed.

Nicholas ignored her as he refilled his teacup, wishing it was something stronger. He added a dollop of cream and stirred, trying to put thoughts of Ella and the glass slippers out of his mind.

"Nicholas, darling." She moved to stand next to him, her tone softening, as she placed a hand on his arm. "Why didn't you ask her to stay?"

He frowned into the tawny liquid. "She seemed homesick, so I never did."

"I don't think she was homesick," she said.

He cut her a sharp glance, his indignation rising. "Then why did you give her the means to return home?"

She dropped her hand. "It was an opportunity for you two to discuss your feelings for each other."

"Feelings, Mother?"

"Yes. I *know* you have them." She gave him a pointed look. "I thought if faced with the real possibility of her leaving Rovenheim, you would ask her stay. Isn't that what you wanted?"

"Yes, of course, Mother. But she—"

"She didn't know how to ask you. I truly think she wanted to, but she was afraid you would turn her down."

He raked a hand through his hair and huffed out a breath. "Why would I refuse her?"

"Because she doesn't know you love her."

He snapped his head in her direction and saw the twinkling of knowledge deep within the blue eyes. Resignation made his shoulders droop.

"We hardly know each other."

"Bah!" She flung her hands up in frustration. "Son, she is the one for you. She has the Spirit of Christmas deep inside her. I saw it in her the first moment I met her. It's why I went to all the trouble of getting you both to that ball."

"So, you *did* have a hand in that!" He wagged an accusatory finger at her.

"Of course, I did. I knew the glass slippers would lead her to her true love." She winked.

He understood his mother was a meddler. He also understood she wanted him to wed and soon because, as she said, she and his father weren't getting any younger. She wanted grandchildren and, beyond that, Rovenheim needed an heir. He, however, did not realize the lengths she would go to make all that happen.

"And they did," she added.

"The legend is true then."

"It's all true. Why do you think Malvina wanted them so badly? She intended to use the power within them to bend our will to hers. She wants nothing more than to rule Rovenheim, but I made sure she would never escape her fortress again."

"You used magic."

"Naturally," she said with a nod. "But all that aside, are you going to take Ella the slippers? Because your constant brooding is really too much." He started to reply when she held up a hand and said, "Let me try again. You *are* going to take Ella the slippers and bring her home."

He grinned. "Yes, Mother. I *am*."

CHAPTER 30

A day after Ella came back from Rovenheim, the family returned in a flourish. They arrived in a magnificent carriage drawn by white horses with a driver and a footman. Ella was busy sweeping the foyer when they all burst through the door and stopped short at the sight of her. Lucinda and Daniella were in front, gaping at her as though she were a stranger.

"What are *you* doing here?" Lucinda asked.

Lillian, her stepmother, shoved them out of the way.

"Why, Ella. You've returned," she said, mustering surprise with a hint of loathing.

Livingstone, who was Lillian's new husband, entered last carrying an oversized suitcase in each hand. He was a tall man with a thick head of hair and a mustache. The rest of his face was clean shaven. He had dark brown eyes under bushy brows. He wore an expensive suit as he stomped into the house.

"Why are we loitering in the foyer?" he growled.

Then he, like the others, stopped short as he noticed Ella for the first time and gaped. She shifted from one foot to the other.

"Who's this?" he asked.

"This is Ella. She was our housemaid before we married, my darling," her stepmother said, waving at her. A sizeable emerald ring winked on her left hand.

"Ah, well. You said you were unable to find help. Perhaps it's good she's returned." He dropped the suitcases. "Bring those up when you have a moment, won't you?"

The girls giggled and charged up the stairs. Lillian followed, giving her a look of contempt as Mr. Livingstone followed her, his hand at the small of her back.

Ella wished then she hadn't bothered to put the bedrooms back in order. She hadn't washed the sheets and remade the beds. She hadn't dusted the rugs and the drapes. Or polished the silver.

She gripped the broom handle so hard, her hand cramped. Then she spun on her heel and stomped back to the kitchen. She dropped the broom, put her face in her hands and forced back the hot tears.

She was nothing but a housemaid now. Not even a member of the family. Even when they were here before, she wasn't a member of the family. Why would now, with their return, be any different?

Soon, they would be clamoring for food. She whisked away the tears, pulled herself together, and started cooking.

A few days went by. Ella lived as a ghost in her own home, pretending to be nothing more than the housemaid and the cook, as was their expectations. Livingstone barely acknowledged her presence. Lucinda and Daniella spent countless hours giving her hateful looks and saying snide things when no one else was around.

Ella was bone tired. Tired of the jeers. Tired of the work. Tired of it all. At night, when she was alone in her uncomfortable bed, she'd take out the vial that brought her home and looked for remnants of fairy dust that could take her back. There wasn't any. Not even a spec. She drifted off to sleep with the throb of loneliness pressing through her. Even in her own home, she felt isolated.

The clock tower bonged it's morning hour. Weary, she pushed off her thin blanket and placed her bare feet on the cold floor, a shiver going up her spine. She glanced at the wool gown and the cloak she still had from Rovenheim. A longing pounded through her. A longing to return. A longing to see Nicholas again.

She wore one of her older gowns instead of ruining all she had left from her adventure. Ingrid was right. It had been a grand adventure.

After dressing, she slipped on her shoes, tied back her hair, and headed down the stairs to the kitchen to begin breakfast for the family before they started ringing the bell demanding. As she prepared the morning tea, there was a knock on the back door. Odd that someone would knock on the back door instead of the front, she thought, as she pulled it open.

An elderly man stood outside wearing nothing but rags. He had a hunched back, an aged face that was a map of wrinkles, thin lips, and stump teeth.

"Oh, 'ello, m'lady," he greeted. "Do ye have anything to give an old poor man like meself? I'm starvin', ye see."

Hesitation went through her. This had happened once before. Before when the box with the slippers appeared and changed her life. She peered at him, trying to see if she knew him, but she didn't. Finally, she nodded.

"One moment."

Back in the kitchen, she wrapped up a loaf of yesterday's bread, some slices of cheese, and a couple of apples. She returned and handed it to him.

"Oh, thank ye, miss. Ye are a kind one to me." He gave her a nod and started to turn.

"Why did you stop here?" she asked.

He turned back, giving her a slanted glance over his shoulder. "I heard talk in the market square there lived a kind young woman here. Thought I'd try me luck." He gave her a grin full of stump, yellowed teeth.

She nodded. Gossip always abounded in the market, especially if Mrs. FitzGerald was involved.

"Where are you headed?" Ella asked.

"Back to the road, m'lady. To make my way south to warmer climes." He gave her another nod of farewell. "Thank ye, again."

"Safe travels, good sir," she called as he headed across the yard.

As she shut the door, she thought no more about the old beggar that called.

The day went along as usual with her polishing the silver, scrubbing the floors and dusting. Snow still dusted the ground, which made the manor drafty and chilly. As she went to the back to bring in more firewood, she heard the unmistakable rumble of hooves and carriage wheels.

Curious, she walked to the side of the house and peered around the corner. She caught a glimpse of a red and gold coach led by eight white chargers. Her heart leapt into her throat as she gasped.

This was different than the one she saw that day in the market when Noella stepped out and they first met. It was larger, more ornate with gold carvings of snowflakes and stars around each door and window. Even the wheels were gold.

Her heart pounded a wicked beat as she hurried into the kitchen, dropped the firewood, and then dashed to the front door. She paused only a moment in the foyer as she caught a glimpse of herself in the mirror. Dirt smudged her face. Hair sprouted around her head making it look untidy. And her gown was dirty from all the cooking and cleaning she'd done.

Nothing to do about that, she thought.

As she turned toward the door, Lucinda pounded down the stairs. Daniella was right behind her.

"Maybe the prince called off his wedding!" Lucinda suggested.

"Maybe he's coming to ask for *my hand*," Daniella said.

"Girls, your manners." Lillian descended the stairs in regal fashion.

None of them noticed Ella standing at the edge of the foyer.

Lucinda was the first to reach the door. She yanked it open just as the man approached with his hand raised to knock.

The man that was the Crown Prince of Rovenheim. He hesitated as surprise washed over his face when he saw Lucinda there.

"Who are you?" she demanded, clearly not expecting a different prince.

He cleared his throat. "I'm here for Miss Ella Rose Tremaine."

Her heart pounded a little harder. Her palms broke into a hot sweat.

"Ella?" Lillian scoffed as she said her name. "Whatever for? She's nothing but a servant girl."

By now, her stepmother reached the bottom of the stairs and moved to stand next to Lucinda, nudging Daniella out of the way.

"She's more than a servant girl," Nicholas said in the snootiest tone she'd ever heard. It made her smile.

Lillian looked him up and down, the disdain on her face. "And just who are you?"

"I am the Crown prince of Rovenheim and I've come for Ella."

"A *prince*," Lucinda breathed. Then she dipped a curtsy. "Forgive my mother, your highness."

His expression said he wasn't interested in her forgiveness. "Where is Ella?"

He hadn't noticed her standing there yet. Ella took in his broad-shouldered appearance. He was dressed in a navy-blue cutaway tailcoat with gold buttons trimmed in trailing gold stars and snowflakes with velvet cuffs and collar. He wore a gold silk cravat, brocade vest, white pants and perfectly polished black boots. His wavy chestnut hair was impeccably combed yet still touched his collar. His bright blue eyes held a certain warmth to them she had longed to see again. He was sigh-worthy and possibly the most distinguished and handsome man she'd ever seen.

Nicholas turned to wave at someone in the coach and, a moment later, Percy arrived by his side caring a velvet pillow with the glass slippers perched on top.

Ella sucked in a sharp breath as she realized what he meant to do.

Everyone turned to stare at her.

Nicholas saw her then. Their eyes met, his sparkling with delight, reflecting his genuine happiness at seeing her again. A surge of warmth spread through her body, filling her with an overwhelming sense of happiness. He was here standing in her house. He had come for her.

He shoved past Lucinda and Lillian, his steps sure-footed as he headed right for her. Percy fell in step behind him carrying the pillow with the slippers.

"What's going on?" Daniella wailed, unable to comprehend what was happening.

Ella knew and hot tears sprang to her eyes. She blinked them away, trying to maintain her composure. It was almost impossible when Nicholas dropped to one knee, taking her hand in his and holding it. His warmth cascaded through her, sending delicious tingles up her spine.

"Ella, you left something behind," he said, the quirk of a grin on his lips.

"Did I?" As she said it, her breath caught in her throat.

He placed his hand behind her left knee, gently lifting her leg. Percy then stepped up and dropped down to remove her shoe.

"What is the meaning of this?" Lillian said, her angry tone lancing right through Ella. "I demand to know—"

"You demand nothing of me, woman," Nicholas shot back.

Lucinda and Daniella both gasped in shock, their heads swiveling to look up at their mother. Lillian's face was a mask of rage as she stood there, hands clasped to her side.

Meanwhile, Percy had removed her worn shoe and slipped on the glass slipper.

"A perfect fit," Nicholas said, his voice quiet as he looked up at her.

He released her leg, giving her an expectant look. She understood and lifted her other foot so Percy could exchange the shoe for the glass slipper. Looking down at them, she still saw the hairline crack in the toe of the right one.

It didn't matter, though. He was here and she had the slippers back.

He rose, taking both of her hands in his and squeezing them.

"Ella, will you return with me?" he asked.

She was nodding before he even finished the question. "Yes. Yes, I will."

"You're not going anywhere." Lillian moved to stand between them and the open door.

But Noella filled up that doorway with her hands on her hips. Her silver hair was twisted into elaborate curls on her head. A spring of holly perched over one ear. She had a fierce look on her face. A look that said not to mess with her or her son.

"She's coming with us and you can't stop her," Noella said.

Lillian turned her face upward, looking down her nose at Noella with such scorn it made Ella's skin crawl. "And *who* are *you?*"

But Noella was not to be intimidated as she stood her ground, peering at each of them with her own brand of condescension.

"The Queen of Rovenheim. The Spirit of Christmas. The one who brings joy and light to all those who deserve it. *None* of you deserve it." She waved her pointed finger to each of them. "Come, darlings, let's leave this place."

Nicholas held her hand tight in his and headed for the door. But Ella remembered something. Something she was unable to leave behind.

"Wait, please. I forgot something."

She tugged her hand out of his grasp and was up the stairs before anyone stopped her. She flung open the door to her bedroom, spotted the small star atop the tree, and hurried toward it. She removed it, holding it a moment, and then placed it in the pocket of her gown. Then she snatched the woolen cloak from the peg by the door, flung it around her shoulders, and left. She didn't even give her room a backward glance.

Back down the stairs, Lillian and her daughters blocked the end of the staircase. Ella halted halfway down. She glanced at Nicholas, her heart ramming hard as she paused there, trying to decide what to do. Fury still pinched Noella's face.

"Move aside," Noella said, a warning tone in her voice.

"She's not leaving here. She's...she's part of the family," Lillian said. Both her daughters gave her shocked looks of disbelief.

"I am not," Ella said. "I'm nothing but the housemaid to you, remember? Now, move aside."

Lillian gave her a hateful glance. "Or what?"

"Or this."

With a wave of her hand, Noella knocked them all out of the way. They crashed together against the wall, sliding to the floor. Ella hurried down the remaining steps, falling into Nicholas's waiting arms. He hugged her tight, taking her hand once again and walking toward the door.

But in the doorway, Ella paused, turning to look once more at her wretch of a stepmother. She pinned her with her gaze.

"Stepmother," she said, slowly and quietly. "I forgive you."

And then, she walked out of the house forever with Nicholas at her side and Noella and Percy behind them.

He held open the door to the coach for her. She climbed in, scooting to the other side of the velvet bench. When he, Noella, and Percy were inside, they took off down the street with the horse's hooves pounding along the cobblestone. Nicholas clutched her hand in his, then kissed it.

"How did you find me?" Ella asked.

"My dear, do you think magic doesn't work here?" Noella said with a smile.

"Earlier today there was an old beggar who came to your kitchen door," Nicholas said. Then he nodded to Percy. "*He* was the beggar."

"Percy?" A laugh bubbled up her throat. "I gave you food!"

"And it was right kind of ye, miss," he said in his beggar accent. They all laughed.

"We visited the market and I talked with some of the people there. The grocer, Mr. Gibson, had quite a lot to say on your behalf, Ella," Noella said.

"Yes, and a Mrs. FitzGerald," Nicholas added.

Ella flushed wondering what the two of them said about her and her situation.

"Perhaps you two should be alone," Noella said. "Percy, shall we?"

"Yes, madam."

And then they were both gone in a puff of glittering fairy dust.

"She does that a lot," Ella said with a giggle. Then she snuggled close to Nicholas.

He wrapped his arm around her shoulders, holding her close. "Why didn't you tell me about your stepmother and how she treated you?"

"I didn't want you to pity me," she said. "And I wasn't sure you wanted me to stay."

"I thought you were homesick and were desperate to leave," he said.

She tilted her head back and looked up at him. "Then we were both wrong."

He nodded. "We were. But I'm here now and I'm taking you away from that woman. What did you forget?"

She sat up straight, pulling the small star out of her pocket. She held it in her palm. "It was my mother's. She always put it on top of the tree when I was a child. It reminded me of the Christmas Star in the village."

He traced the lines of the star with a fingertip. "It will have its own unique place in the castle, then."

Tears clouded her vision. She blinked them away as she tucked it back into her pocket.

He slipped his hand over her cheek, caressing it with his thumb. "You left the slippers."

"I didn't mean to. I was going to tell you but never got the chance."

"I thought you didn't want to be with me," he said.

"That could not be further from the truth," she whispered. "I'm glad you came for me. I missed you. I missed everyone."

"I missed you, too, Ella. And..." He paused, pressing his forehead against hers and cupping her face. "I love you."

Her heart skipped a happy beat. "I love you, too."

He kissed her. A sweet kiss that only lasted a moment. When she pulled away, she looked up into those beautiful blue eyes and smiled.

"Take me home to Rovenheim, Nicholas."

He grinned. "As my lady commands."

Epilogue

"The end," Hilde said, smiling broadly.

Marigold gave a wistful sigh as she burrowed deeper under the blankets. "Did they live happily ever after?"

She smiled, thinking of Ella and Nicholas and how happy she was to live inside the grand castle. "They did."

"Did they get married in the castle?" she asked around a yawn.

It was a Christmas wedding, naturally, with the castle hall decked in boughs of holly from top to bottom. Noella spared no expense. Ella's gown was the most beautiful white gown with a long cathedral length train that sparkled with shimmering crystals embroidered along it. The bodice was covered in a delicate lace. She wore an elaborate tiara attached to a veil that was the same length as her gown. Her bouquet was made up of winter flowers that included red and white roses, holly berries, snowdrops, and greenery. The entire village of Rovenheim turned out for the festive affair. Nicholas wore a white suit with long tails, shiny black boots, and a sprig of holly in his lapel like the night they met at the Christmas ball.

This was all too much to tell her niece, so she simply said, "They certainly did." Hilde rose and tucked the blankets around her. "Now, it's time to sleep so Santa can come."

"But I'm not sleepy." And despite her protest, she yawned.

"You are. Goodnight, sweet girl." Hilde kissed her forehead. "May sugar plums dance in your head."

"Night-night, auntie."

Hilde turned for the door. As her hand wrapped around the knob, Marigold had one more question.

"Auntie, was Nicholas's father Santa Claus?"

Smiling, she turned back to her niece. "Some call him that. But in Rovenheim, they call him Father Christmas."

That seemed to satisfy the girl. She smiled, closed her eyes, and rolled to her side. Hilde turned off her light and exited the room, closing the door softly behind her.

The seed had been planted. Now, she was excited to watch it grow.

Acknowledgements

No book is possible without help. I am fortunate to have a support group that helps me, even if it's just to listen to me work through plot details.

First, to my sister, **Kathy,** who reads everything I write and helps proofread. I'm a perfectionist, so it really bothers me when there are typos!

Also, thanks to **Jennifer August** for the margarita lunches and all the writing talk. And a big thanks for doing a read-through of this to also help catch those pesky typos.

To **my husband** for all his patience and support. I disappear every night for at least an hour to write and get these stories out of my head. He is the best.

And to you, **readers**, who read my books and support this indie author. It means the world to me.

I thoroughly enjoyed writing this retelling of Cinderella. It makes me happy. I hope it does you, too.

Also by Michelle Miles

Age of Wizards (Epic Fantasy)

In the Tower of the Wizard King

On the Hunt for the Wizard King

Dragon Protectors (Paranormal Shifter Romance)

Desiring the Dragon Lord

Seducing the Dragon Knight

Tempting Her Dragon Bodyguard

Dragon Protectors Book Collection, Books 1-3

Dream Walker (Urban Fantasy)

Call of the Dark

Blood and Bone

Flame and Fury

Smoke and Ashes

Light of the World

Dream Walker Collection (Books 1-5)

Dream Walker: Origins (Fantasy)

Provenance

Enchanted Realms (Fantasy Romance)

Once Upon a Midnight Clear

Once Upon True Love's Kiss

Once Upon an Enchanted Kiss

Five Towers (YA Fantasy)

The Sorcerer's Daughter

**Ransom & Fortune Adventures
(Time Travel Action/Adventure)**

Highland Fling, Vol 1

Dead of Winter, Vol 2

The Citadel, Vol 3

Lord of the Underworld, Vol 4

Realm of Honor (Fantasy Romance)

One Knight Only

Only for a Knight

A Knight to Remember

A Knight Like No Other

Shadows of the Knight

Realm of Honor Collection (Books 1-5)

Guardians of Atlantis (Fantasy Romance)

Tempting Eden

Seducing Eve

Ravishing Helene

Guardians of Atlantis Box Set

Shorts and Anthologies (Fantasy/Paranormal)

A Dance Among the Faeries, Short Story

Eorwulf, Short Story

The Soul of Sharah, Short Story

Sinfully Sweet, Short Story

Flights of Fantasy: A Collection of Short Stories

ABOUT THE AUTHOR

MICHELLE MILES believes in fairy tales, true love and magic. She writes heart-stopping urban fantasy, epic fantasy and paranormal romance with an action/adventure twist that will leave you breathless. She is the author of numerous series that includes everything from angels and demons to fairies, dragons and elves.

She is a member of Romance Writers of America (RWA) and Science Fiction and Fantasy Writers Association (SFWA). A native Texan, in her spare time she loves reading, listening to music, watching movies, hiking, and drinking wine. She can be found online at Facebook, Instagram, Pinterest and Goodreads.

Your Adventure Awaits

Read more at MichelleMiles.net